OUR PERFECT MOMENT

The McCormicks
Book 6

ELENA AITKEN

Chapter One

AMBER

I NAVIGATED my rental car onto the side of the road under the sign that announced I was entering Crystal Creek. What the sign didn't say, but what was evident by the landscape, was that the town was in the middle of nowhere. Or, more specifically, what looked to be the middle of a frosty field in Northern Saskatchewan. I still couldn't figure out why my best friend had decided this was an up-and-coming market to flip houses, but I wasn't there to pass judgment. I was there to visit my friend and have a little break from my life.

I pulled my cell phone out of my purse and powered it on. I made it a rule never to drive with my phone on in case I was tempted to look at it. Not only was distracted driving incredibly dangerous, it was also against the law in most places now, and I was definitely a rule follower. I was proud of the fact that I'd never broken a law. Ever. I didn't even have a parking ticket on my record. And I would happily keep it that way.

Immediately, the screen lit up with missed texts and calls. No surprise—most of them were from my friend, and former roommate, Josie Price. I ignored the voicemails and dialed Josie's number.

My friend answered on the first ring.

"Seriously," Josie said. "It wouldn't kill you to keep your phone on."

"No," I answered smoothly. "But it could kill someone else. What's up? I just got to town." It had taken me all day to fly halfway across the country from Toronto, rent a car, and drive out into some farmer's field, but I'd made it.

"Oh no." Josie groaned.

"Oh yes." I ignored the prickle of concern that popped up. I wasn't going to let anything ruin this trip. I'd finally planned something spontaneous, and I was going to enjoy every minute of catching up with my friend. The irony that I'd planned a spontaneous trip wasn't lost on me, but for me, leaving on a mostly unplanned vacation to visit a friend in the middle of nowhere in Saskatchewan, when what I really should be doing was figuring out what firms to apply to if I wasn't offered the position I was so sure I'd get, was out of character. Way out of character. Besides, I should have already been offered the job. The panic that I'd been fighting for the last week, since not getting the call about the job when I'd expected it, started to well up again, but I swallowed hard and focused on Josie.

One problem at a time. And it did seem as if Josie were about to present me a problem. I had a feeling I was going to regret my only slightly planned and very spontaneous trip by my standards.

"Remember?" I said the word slowly. "That was the plan." I took a breath and squeezed my eyes shut tight. "Please tell me you remembered I was coming." I loved Josie like a sister, but to say my friend was a bit scatterbrained would be a major understatement. It definitely wouldn't be the first time Josie totally spaced on our plans.

"Of course I remembered."

"Good." Relief washed over me, but it only lasted a moment.

"Only I'm not there."

Panic punched me in the gut. "What?" I took a deep breath and then another. I focused on breathing in through my nose and out through my mouth just like my yoga teacher had taught me. I'd been working hard on not letting myself get worked up by small things. Or anything. It was still a work in progress to be sure, as I still found my stress level rising in the smallest of situations. But this situation isn't small. I exhaled hard. "Where are you, Josie?"

"Well…here's the thing."

"Where are you?"

"Vancouver."

"Vancouver? Why are you in Vancouver?"

"Well, more specifically, a suburb of Vancouver. And honestly, it's not that big of a deal. I'll be back in a few days, and we'll hang out just like we planned. If I could have done anything about it, I would have. But I have a property here that I was renting, and the renters left without any notice, and the place is in shambles. I need to fix it up and get it organized to rent again before I lose more money on it. I really am sorry, Amber. I promise I'll be there in a few days, and—"

"When?" I needed something specific because if it was going to be too long, I could get back on a plane and—do what? For the first time in my life, I had nowhere to go. Without the job offer, there was nothing for me in Toronto. All of my things, what little I had, were in storage. For the first time in my life, I didn't have a plan, and that scared the hell out of me. But I couldn't get worked up. At least not yet.

"I promise it will only be a few days at most," Josie was

saying. "I have some people lined up to help me out and an agency that will handle the rental. It shouldn't take too long."

Josie had been my roommate for our first two years of college before Josie had dropped out to join the real estate market. She'd actually been fairly successful, even with the bust of the market. She attributed her success to her personal involvement and her knack for finding up-and-coming markets that were mostly overlooked by the bigger firms. Which was why she was in Crystal Creek. The local economy was starting to rebound from the recession and was becoming a hot market for young couples who wanted a small-town feel to raise their families in. She'd found herself a little house in desperate need of a facelift, and although the physical labor didn't appeal to me in any way, a tiny town— tucked away from everybody and everything—did. At least for a few days. If I had no place to go, nowhere was a good place to be.

"I promise I'll be back as soon as I can," Josie said. "Don't even think about leaving before I get there."

How did she know that had been my first thought?

Because she knows me better than anyone. I would have laughed at myself and the situation I found myself in if I weren't so freaked out. "Josie, I can't just stay in a strange town. I don't even have a—"

"Oh my goodness," my friend interrupted me. "Of course you can. Crystal Creek is like the safest town ever. There's zero crime, and I bet you'll be there not even five minutes before someone knocks on the door with fresh-baked muffins. The key is under the pot next to the door."

I shook my head and forced myself to bite back the response that was on the tip of my tongue. It wasn't 1968; you couldn't just leave your doors open or keys under flowerpots. There were people who… I forced myself to take another deep breath.

"Don't be all weird about it, Amber," Josie continued, as if she could hear my thoughts.

"I'm not."

Josie laughed. "Right. Well, trust me. There's not really even a reason to lock the door at all, but it's what everyone there does."

"If everyone does it, you might as well not lock the door at all."

"That's exactly what I'm saying." My friend laughed again. "Look, I have to go, but make yourself at home, okay? I put a pile of blankets on the couch, or you can stay in my room. There are fresh towels in the bathroom. Whatever you need, help yourself."

I sighed. I knew enough to know when I'd been beat. Besides, I was tired and the thought of driving all the way back to the city, sitting at the airport, and hoping for another flight out…well, it was just easier to spend the night. "Okay."

"You'll be fine, Amber. Besides, I know you, and I know you need a little time to think things through. Consider this time alone a little gift, a chance to sort things out."

Josie really did know me better than anyone. I smiled and nodded. "Love you. See you soon."

I hung up the phone and immediately powered it off before I stuck it back into my purse. I looked at the directions I'd printed out. Josie's house was just on the edge of the small town. It shouldn't take me too long to get there. Thankfully, the roads weren't too snow-covered. In fact, there wasn't much snow at all for the middle of November. Not that I had spent much time in Saskatchewan, but I'd anticipated it to be a lot colder, with a lot more snow.

I tilted the rearview mirror down so I could see my reflection. "Pull yourself together, Amber." I took a deep breath. "You don't need to be in control. Just trust. You will be fine."

It was silly. Ridiculous, really, but it was a mantra I'd been repeating to myself for the last few days ever since I'd decided to go "off plan" for a little bit. If Josie had heard me, she would have laughed because she'd been telling me that for years. But I didn't care. Because as much as I loved my best friend, Josie didn't understand my need for control. She never had. But then again, Josie's whole world hadn't been blown up when she was young. At a time when my family life was spinning out of control, the only thing I actually had any say in was managing all of the day-to-day details of my life. So I did.

And it had worked, too. For a while.

But more and more, I had been feeling as though something needed to change.

I was stuck. I'd been stuck for a long time. And although I had no idea how to get unstuck, I did know that I couldn't keep doing what I'd been doing.

Something needed to change.

The problem was, I still didn't know what.

COLE

I WAS sure my little sister wouldn't mind if I crashed at her house. Well, I was pretty sure Josie wouldn't mind. After all, she'd invited me. The fact that I'd screwed up on the dates and was a few weeks earlier than I'd told her I was coming wouldn't be a big deal.

Probably.

Either way, it didn't matter because she wasn't home when I let myself in the front door with the key I'd guessed to be under the flowerpot on the front porch. I'd laughed when Josie told me she was doing a flip in a tiny town in Saskatchewan. It didn't really seem like a hotbed for real estate, but just driving through the little town of Crystal Creek, even a guy like me, who was anti everything quaint and small town, could agree that it was probably a good investment. The town was cute, like a made-for-television movie. There seemed to be a handful of new businesses on the main street, and people were walking around everywhere. Picturesque was the word that came to mind—some people liked that. I wasn't one of them, but I did like my little sister, and after almost two years of backpacking and working in Australia, I actually missed her.

I unlocked the front door with a click and hauled my backpack and the one small bag of supplies that I'd stopped at the store for inside. Josie told me the house needed a lot of work—most flips did—but she'd insisted that this one was livable. My plan was to live in the house for a few months while I did the needed repairs. I had only taken a total of three steps into the house, but that was all I needed to see to know that the work would take longer than a few months.

The exterior paint was peeling badly, and I'd counted more than one shutter hanging askew. Never mind what I'd find when I looked a little closer at the roof and gutters. Although the outside was one thing, the inside was a whole other thing altogether.

I didn't bother to take my boots off as I walked across the seventies gold-flecked linoleum into the kitchen, where I was greeted with more seventies influence in the way of mustard-yellow appliances and matching golden oak cupboards and Formica countertops.

"Wow." I shook my head with a laugh as I opened the fridge to put my beer inside. "At least it works," I said. "There's nothing worse than warm beer." And since I was on the subject...I grabbed a can from the six-pack before I put it on the empty shelf inside.

I'd already been back in Canada, traveling for almost two

weeks. I'd spent my time visiting old friends and paid an obligatory visit to my parents. I suffered through the guilt-filled conversations about how Dad was slowing down and could really use some help in the shop, so he didn't have to work so hard. Just like every time I spoke with my parents, I tried to plant the suggestion that they just go ahead and sell the family store. Hell, it was more than a suggestion; I'd come right out and said it more than once.

Mostly, I just wanted to visit with Josie. Despite our two-year age difference, we'd always been close. I would have been happier to spend more time with my little sister, but she'd been so busy with her flipping business. I'd take what I could get before I headed back to Sydney, hopefully before Christmas. Australia would be even better than it already was if it weren't so damned far away. Although the fact that it was on the other side of the world had definitely been one of the selling features of buying the original plane ticket almost two years earlier. The farther I could get from my family, their expectations, and a life of responsibility and predictability, the better. And it had worked, too.

The irony of it was that now that my parents had finally started to accept that I was never going to live the life that they wanted me to, I was starting to change my mind. Living and working in Australia had been everything I thought it would be. I worked when I needed to, loved when I wanted to, and moved on when it was time. But more and more, I'd been thinking that maybe there was something more out there.

I just didn't know what it was.

Hopefully, a little time with my sister would help me sort out what my next step would be. I hadn't seen her since the last time I'd crashed on her couch when she was still in college, right before I'd left. We were definitely overdue for a catch-up. And by the looks of things, Josie would be able to use my help for a few days, too.

With my beer in hand, I walked through the house, taking a mental inventory of what needed to be done. The tour didn't take long, and when I was done investigating the upstairs, which really only had one usable room at the moment, considering the others were full of fixtures, boxes, and cans of paint, I plopped down on the couch. At least Josie had a little bit of furniture and a TV. I flicked on the television and flipped through the channels until I found a football game. It didn't matter who was playing, especially because within thirty minutes, I could barely keep my eyes open. I managed to flick the television off before I stretched out and fell asleep in the dark room.

Chapter Two

AMBER

DESPITE THE EARLY EVENING HOUR, it was already dark by the time I pulled up to the little house. I'd made the last-minute decision to stop at the grocery store in town to pick up a few supplies to get me through the night. I was looking forward to a hot shower and a quiet night in.

With the grocery bag balanced in one arm, I pulled my suitcase behind me and up onto the porch. Using the light from my cell phone, I found the key under the flowerpot, just the way Josie said I would. I opened the door and tucked the key back into my pocket. There was no way I was putting it back under there. It was ridiculous to leave a key to my home right there on the porch where anyone who happened to be walking by could get it. Especially considering Josie said everyone in town did it.

Craziness. And there was no way I would have anything to

do with that kind of blatant disregard for my own personal safety.

I made my way into the little house, left my suitcase by the front door, and took the bag into the kitchen, where I unloaded the few things I bought. I opened the retro fridge to put my orange juice inside, but there wasn't much in there, which was a bit concerning for me. Wasn't Josie eating properly? She never did. She was always so thin, but could survive on potato chips and beer. Speaking of beer…

I eyed the beer in the fridge. It had been a long time since I'd let myself indulge in alcohol. Five months, three weeks, and two days to be exact. Not that I was counting, because I really wasn't. But I remembered the last time I'd had any alcohol at all, because my boyfriend Randy had bought a bottle of champagne to celebrate my graduation from college. The bubbles had tingled and popped on my tongue, and two glasses had made my head fuzzy, but not so fuzzy that I didn't sober up immediately when he broke up with me by telling me he didn't want to settle down to a boring and predictable life.

And that's all I offered.

We'd dated for over two years. I thought he was going to propose that night. After all, it was the next logical step. I'd graduated from school. Marriage should be next.

Logical. Everything I did was always logical. Planned. Organized. Despite the fact that he was an asshole about it, Randy was right. Life with me would have been boring and predictable. I couldn't blame him for not wanting that. Heck, I didn't want that. And it was my life. His leaving had been a shock to be sure, but I could honestly say that I didn't miss his presence. Which not only told me everything I needed to know about the relationship, but also gave me a bit of a shove in the right—hopefully less logical—direction.

I grabbed a beer and cracked it open. I was done with being

boring and predictable. Before I put it to my lips, I paused and grabbed a tea towel to give the can a wipe. Okay, I wasn't totally done with being predictable and boring, but I was working on it.

I'd spent the last few months finishing my internship in Toronto at Wallace and McKwade, the accounting firm I'd expected to be offered a job at. I'd been so sure that I'd get the job that I hadn't even bothered to apply anywhere else. A move that I was regretting more and more every day. Because the offer hadn't come. And now, instead of being excited about the possibility of working at Wallace and McKwade, I was nervous and uncertain. Six months ago—heck, even a month ago—I would have jumped at the opportunity to stay in Toronto and take the job, but I couldn't deny that Randy's words to me had sunk in.

Boring and predictable.

Is that all life had to offer?

I took a deep drink of my beer, grimacing a little at the sour taste. I'd never been a big beer drinker. It was all too much to think about for one night.

"One thing at a time," I told myself. After all, I'd just taken a plane halfway across the country, to a strange town in the middle of nowhere, to visit a friend who wasn't even there. If I were looking to burst out of my comfort zone, I'd done enough bursting for one day. There would be nothing wrong with sitting in front of the television and doing a bunch of nothing for the rest of the night.

Surely Josie had a television.

I took my beer and the packaged salad I'd bought at the store, and made my way into the room I assumed would be the living room. I flicked the light switch.

Nothing.

Of course. Electrical was probably on the list of things Josie would be fixing. Hopefully, the TV would work.

With my hands full, I did my best to navigate my way

through the room. My shin bumped into the coffee table. I set my beer and salad down and picked up the remote control I felt next to it. When I clicked it, the screen came on and illuminated the room enough for me to back up and plop down on the couch.

"Oomph! What the hell?"

I screamed as I jumped up. "Whoever you are..." My eyes wide, I pressed my back against the wall, wielded the remote in my hand like a weapon, and turned to see whatever—or more likely, whoever—had made the noise when I'd sat on what was decidedly not a couch. "You're trespassing," I continued, keeping my voice as steady as I could. "And I have a weapon." I wielded the remote in my hand like the weapon I didn't have and crouched into an attack position as I focused on the form on the couch.

As I watched, the man unfolded himself and got to his feet. He raised his hands in the air. "I'm not going to—"

"Don't move! Stay right—Cole?" I took a step back until I bumped into the wall. If running had been an option, I would have turned and run all the way back to Ontario. But running wasn't an option because my body had gone from shock to fear to...full-on arousal.

———————

COLE

I BLINKED ONCE and then again, hard. I'd been having a very nice dream that involved the Australian beach, a surfboard, and a woman in a very small bikini. Being woken by someone sitting on me wasn't exactly the way I'd been hoping that particular dream would end.

The voice sounded familiar, but in my sleepy fog, I didn't quite register who was staring at me, threatening me with... a remote control?

"Cole Price? What the hell are you doing here?"

And there it was. The icy formalness that could only be Josie's old roommate. "Amber."

"Yes. Who else would it be?"

I pulled myself to a sitting position and scratched at the scruff on my face. It had been at least a few weeks since I'd shaved. "Well, I don't know," I said. "For starters, I might have been expecting my little sister." I rubbed at my face, trying to wake myself up completely. "This is my house, after all."

Amber scowled, but I could see the flush working its way up her neck. I tried not to smile, but I remembered very well the effect I'd had on my little sister's roommate two years ago when I'd visited. The attraction wasn't entirely one-sided, not by a long shot, not that I'd ever admit that out loud. She was my sister's friend, and she had a boyfriend. A particularly stuck-up douchebag, if I remembered correctly. But still, it wasn't my style to get involved with unavailable women.

"Josie isn't here." Amber's voice trembled just a little. "You should know that."

I shook my head. "Nope. Didn't know that."

"Then why are you here?"

I chuckled. "My sister's house. Remember?"

The flush moved up to her cheeks. But it wasn't Amber's cheeks that I was looking at. It was where the heated skin disappeared beneath her sweater, which pulled tightly over her currently heaving chest. My cock twitched. Damn, she was definitely hot in that stick up your ass, wound up tighter than a top kinda way.

"That doesn't explain why you're here." She jabbed the remote in my direction.

I moved to stand, but Amber's gestures with the remote got

a little wilder, so I held up my hands in surrender. "Okay, I'll sit. But you should too. And put that remote down before you hurt someone. I come in peace, I promise." I stopped myself before adding something crude that she probably wouldn't appreciate. Too many months spent on an Australian cattle ranch had left me a little rougher around the edges than usual.

I didn't really think she'd sit down, but to my surprise, she did. In a hardback chair across the room. Far away from me. The remote control was still clutched in her hand, but at least it wasn't pointed at me anymore.

"Amber, I'm not going to hurt you. You know me."

She looked as if she were going to say something, but then her face turned an even brighter shade of red, and she shook her head. "Tell me why you're here," she said after a moment. "Josie invited me to stay with her for a few days, and I just spoke with her. She didn't tell me you'd be coming, and I know she would have mentioned it. She knows how I like to…"

She let the sentence trail away, but she didn't need to finish it. Amber had always been the planner type. The exact opposite of Josie, and me, for that matter. I wasn't surprised that she was thrown off by my appearance. And now that I thought of it…the fact that Amber had a trip planned was probably the very reason Josie told me not to come for a few more weeks when I'd called the other day. My sister wasn't stupid. She would have seen the way her roommate had reacted to my big brother when we'd been together the last time. And as much as she loved me, there was no doubt that Josie thought I would be a bad influence on her straight-laced friend.

I laughed a little to myself at the ridiculous idea. But when I looked across the room at Amber—at the way her breath was still coming a little too quick, and the sexy flush that was starting to fade a bit—a very recognizable flash of desire fired low in my gut.

Maybe Josie had a reason to be concerned after all?

I cleared my throat and forced all dirty thoughts out of my mind. At least for the moment. "I arrived a little earlier than planned," I said. "But don't worry, I'm only here for a short visit and then back to Australia. Now, since you seem to have more information than I do, are you going to tell me where my sister is?"

"Right." Amber, clearly resigned to the fact that I wasn't going anywhere for the moment, reached forward and exchanged the remote control for the beer on the coffee table. "She's in Vancouver to fix up a rental she had that went bad. It was last-minute, and she should be back in a few days. So maybe if you came back then, you'll be able to—"

"I'm not going anywhere."

She paused, the beer halfway to her lips. "You have to."

"No, I don't."

"But I'm here."

"And?"

"You can't be here when I'm here."

I laughed out loud. "Why not? You seem to be perfectly comfortable helping yourself to my beers." I pointed at the can in her hand. "Why not with my presence?"

She quickly put the can on the table and sat up, her back stiffer than ever.

"You can drink it."

She shook her head and must have realized she was being ridiculous because she quickly added, "Thank you. And, just so you know, I'm not uncomfortable with you being here."

I tilted my head and raised my eyebrow.

"I'm not," she insisted. "I was just a little bit unprepared, is all."

"A little bit?"

"Okay…a lot." She picked up the beer again and took a drink this time. "But really, if you could just come back after I leave…"

"I have nowhere else to go, sweetheart. So it looks like you're stuck with me."

AMBER

SWEETHEART? Sweetheart?!

Who did he think he was, calling me a name like that?

Needing a little space to think, I disappeared into the kitchen. I couldn't just sit there across from him like that. Not when he was looking at me with those eyes. Those green eyes that always seemed to look straight past every wall I'd ever put up.

I opened the fridge, practically threw my prepackaged salad inside, and slammed it shut again.

Sweetheart.

Dammit.

The worst part was, I'd liked it when he'd called me that. A lot. The word had sparked some kind of full-body reaction, and I knew I was blushing again. Cole had that effect on me. He always had. Well, the only other time I'd met him, anyway. But that had been enough to fuel my dreams for months. Okay, longer than months. I'd just started dating Randy when Cole came to visit Josie. I felt guilty even now remembering the way I used to think about what it would have felt like to have Cole's hands on me instead of Randy's, his lips on—no!

I needed to stop that. I couldn't allow myself to think about Cole like that. Not again. Absolutely nothing good could come out of that. Especially with him in the next room.

"Are you hungry?" His deep, slightly Australian-accented voice called from the living room.

Was I hungry? Was I hungry? If the way my body was

vibrating was any indication, the answer was yes. Hell yes. I was really damn hungry.

"No," I replied, keeping my voice as steady as possible. "Not even a little."

"Well, I'm starving."

I whipped around to see him leaning against the doorjamb, looking even sexier than he had been lying on the couch. How was that even possible?

"Let's go into town and get some food. I saw a pub when I was coming through. I bet they have wings."

At the mention of a little deep-fried goodness, my stomach growled. When was the last time I'd indulged in something like pub food? I usually stick to salads and chicken breasts. Wings would be good. But going out with Cole? That probably wasn't a good idea. No, it wouldn't be a good idea at all.

He must have seen me waver, because he added, "Come on. My treat. Besides, it'll give us a chance to discuss the arrangements here. I'm sure you'll want a plan."

Was he teasing me?

Yes. One look at the cocky, but admittedly very sexy smile on his face, told me that he was definitely teasing me. But it didn't slip my notice that he remembered that detail about me. Had he thought about me at all over the years?

I almost laughed out loud at the ridiculousness of that thought. Why on earth would Cole Price ever have given a second thought to his little sister's uptight roommate, who he had met briefly two years ago?

The thought was hilarious. But wings actually did sound like a pretty good idea. And teasing or not, Cole was right: I was going to need a plan. Or, in the interest of trying not to overplan everything, I needed some idea of what we were going to do because it certainly didn't seem as if either of us would be leaving.

"Okay," I agreed after a moment. "But give me a minute to freshen up. It's been a long day."

"Take all the time you need."

He didn't move from the doorway, so I had to walk directly past him, turning to the side to squeeze by. "Excuse me." He grinned, but only stepped back slightly. Despite my best effort to avoid him, my breast brushed his chest, and the zing of electricity between us almost dropped me to my knees. I couldn't be sure how, but somehow I kept walking and grabbed my suitcase.

"Amber?"

I froze, my hand on my bag.

"Just for the record," he continued when I didn't turn around. "I don't think you need any time at all to freshen up. You look great."

Chapter Three

AMBER

"JOSIE, ANSWER THE PHONE." I held my phone tight to my ear and looked around my friend's bedroom. I hadn't known where else to go to freshen up. There were no other usable spare rooms and there was no way I could stay down there with him. "Josie, pick up…pick up…pick—" I paced the floor of the tiny space in an effort to slow my heart rate, to calm my mind, to…stop thinking about those eyes and the way they looked at me.

Dammit.

I was in so much trouble.

I was just about to hang up when finally my friend's voice came across the line. "Amber? Are you—"

"What the hell, Josie?" I didn't waste any time getting right to the point. "You didn't tell me your brother was going to be here."

"Cole?"

"Is there another one?"

God help me if there were more than one.

"What's he doing there?"

"You tell me."

"He's not supposed to be visiting for a few weeks. Christmas. I was going to have him help me out while he was here, but I was hoping to enjoy a bit of time with you before he came to—"

"Well, he's here now." I stopped pacing and stared at myself in the mirror. My blonde hair was disheveled from travel, and had started to unravel from my tight French braid. The effect left me looking slightly wild, at least by my standards. But not as wild as the look in my eyes. Is that what Cole did to me?

Was that a bad thing?

"Oh."

"Yes. Oh."

"Okay, well, it's not ideal, but—"

"Right?" I exhaled with relief. Thank goodness Josie realized that it was definitely not okay that Cole was there with me.

"I'll send him a text right now."

"Thank you, Josie." I worked it out in my head. Josie would text him and tell him that he had to leave. I could get through one night with him in the house, and he'd be gone in the morning.

"He can get started with a few things before I get back."

"I just think it's better if he's not—wait." I froze again. "What did you say? Get started?"

"Yes. With the house," Josie said. "I mean, it's not ideal that he arrived while I'm not there, but I really do need his help with a few things, so I might as well—"

"You want him to stay?" I realized I sounded ridiculous. Of course, Josie wanted her brother to stay.

"Of course I do," she said, as if she'd just read my mind.

"He's my brother, Amber. Is that okay? I mean, there's no problem with him being there, is there?"

I couldn't be sure, but I could have sworn there was a trace of suspicion in Josie's voice. There was no way I could explain to my best friend that I found her older brother intensely, dangerously sexy. Like, to the point of distraction, sexy. The kind of sexy that could get me into serious trouble. No. I absolutely could not tell Josie that. "No," I said quickly. "There's no problem. At all."

I hoped my voice sounded a whole lot more relaxed than I felt.

"Oh, good, because this trip is going to put me behind with my timeline, and if I can't get this house sorted out quickly, I don't know what I'm going to do. I need the rental income to get the Crystal Creek house finished. Can you ask him to call me when he has a second?"

"I'll tell him."

"Great, because I was hoping to be out of here by tomorrow, but now the carpet is…anyway, it doesn't matter. I could actually really use Cole here, but as long as he's in Crystal Creek, I might as well use his talents on that house, right?"

"Right." I agreed, although my mind immediately went to a different kind of talent I was sure Cole possessed. The kind of talent that I couldn't help but be very interested in.

Josie prattled on for a few more minutes about how things were going with the house repairs in Vancouver. I put her on speakerphone and only half listened as I changed into a fresh blouse from my suitcase and brushed my hair out before tying it back into a tight braid.

"I'm really sorry, Amber." The shift in conversation caught my attention, and I picked up the phone again.

"For what?"

"I know how you don't like surprises," Josie said, her voice sincere. "I know with everything over the last few months, this must be—"

"It's fine," I cut her off as I assessed my reflection in the mirror.

"It is?"

"It really is." It wasn't a total lie. After all, I had told myself that things had to change. Boring and predictable were out. New and spontaneous were in. Maybe the more I said it, even to myself, the more I'd actually start to believe it. "I'm trying something new."

"Really? Then maybe you'd like to—"

I laughed at the skepticism in my friend's voice and cut off her idea before it could take root. "I said I was trying something new, Josie. One step at a time, okay?"

COLE

LESS THAN AN HOUR LATER, Amber and I were seated in a faded red plush-lined booth in the back of the only pub in town, the Tipping Cow. There wasn't much to it, but the music was good and the beer was cold, and as far as I was concerned, those were the two most important things for a night out in a small town. Aside from the company, of course. "To us." I raised my mug of beer and waited for Amber to join me in the toast. To my surprise, I didn't have to wait long.

"To us," she repeated. "Although I have absolutely no idea why we would toast to us."

She took a sip of her beer. Another surprise for me. When I'd offered to order a jug of draft, I thought for sure she'd want to order a glass of white wine or a martini or something. She was full of surprises. Not that she shouldn't be. After all, we barely knew each other, and spending a few days in someone's apartment two years earlier didn't mean I knew anything about her at all.

But dammed if I didn't want to know everything there was to know. Something about her buttoned-down, scared-to-jump, uptight schoolmarm look that she had going on made me want to know a whole lot more about her. More specifically, what exactly was hiding under that hard shell?

"We're toasting to us," I said after my own sip of beer, "because we're here. Together. And if that isn't a reason to toast, I'm not sure what is."

"Oh." She blushed and kind of half choked on her beer before her fingers came up to her mouth, and I had to force myself not to stare. "I didn't—"

"I know you didn't expect, or maybe even want, this." I cut her off smoothly. "But that's what we've got and I, for one, don't think it's such a bad thing."

She tipped her head and examined me for a moment. "You don't?"

"No. Not at all. In fact, I can't think of a better way to spend a few days before Josie gets home than with her best friend." I actually could. I could think of a whole lot more specific ways to spend the time with her—notably in bed, or up against a wall. I wasn't picky. But I was pretty sure if I said those things out loud, she'd either slap me in the face or turn around and run out of there. Neither of which was something I wanted.

As it was, Amber blushed. But her blouse was buttoned up all the way to the collar, and I was robbed of seeing the sexy, warm skin on her neck that I knew was hiding under the thin fabric.

"Don't tell me you can think of something better, then?" I challenged her. "Because this seems pretty good to me."

The tension between us was thick, but not uncomfortable. Quite the opposite. I liked it. Because a sexual tension that strong meant only one thing: the release—when it finally came—would be dynamite. That being said, Amber wasn't like the other women I usually flirted with, and for a moment, I worried that maybe I'd pushed her too far, too fast. Amber was definitely the type who would spook easily. Like a frightened kitten. It was entirely possible she would run and hide. But I could see a strength in her, too, and I was counting on the glimmer of a tiger inside that would keep her from running. Because despite the fact that I'd like to get a little closer, I meant it when I said I couldn't think of anything better than spending time with her. I couldn't. After a few weeks of couch surfing with old friends with whom I'd completely run out of things in common, and dealing with my parents, flirting with Amber for a few days would be a very welcome distraction.

Before Amber could answer properly, the waitress arrived and slid a basket of wings between us. Amber sat back and smiled at the woman, thanking her, and just like that, the tension between us was broken. She grabbed one of the wings and bit into it.

"I thought you weren't hungry?" I laughed and chose a wing of my own.

A moment later, she tossed the bones on a plate. "I was wrong." Her voice was low and unlike what I'd heard before. "I'm actually quite hungry." She watched me with heavy-lidded eyes, and when she put her finger in her mouth and slowly—oh so slowly that I wished I were that finger—licked it clean, I finally realized what she was talking about.

I sat back, my chicken wing forgotten, trying to process what had just happened. So much for frightened little kitten. She'd transformed in front of my eyes in a millisecond. It was a transformation I wasn't entirely sure I trusted, but it was interesting for sure. I reached across the table and took her hand.

"Why don't we start with wings and beer and see where it goes?"

Just as I expected her to, Amber stiffened slightly, giving herself away. Welcome back, little kitten. I chuckled a little to myself and released her hand. "It's okay, Amber. I'm not going to bite." Ironically, I had to bite my tongue to keep from adding, Not unless you want me to. That would be way too much, way too soon.

She didn't respond, but instead went back to the wings. This time, she ate a little less seductively, using her napkin to wipe her fingers. It was disappointing to be sure, but I forced myself not to stare. I waited a few minutes before I shifted the conversation to a much safer topic. "So, what have you been up to for the last few years? Unlike my sister, I assume you stayed in school."

"Why would you assume that?" Her voice hardened, and she stiffened her shoulders. "Because I seem like the school type? The super predictable type?"

"Whoa." I held up my hands in defense as I clearly hit a nerve. "I didn't mean anything by it at all. It's just that Josie dropped out, and I would hope, or think anyway, that most people have a little more common sense than her when it comes to things like their future."

"Do you?" she challenged. "Have more sense than her?"

I laughed. "Good point. I suppose as the big brother, I don't set the best example myself."

I hadn't even graduated from post-secondary. I'd finished a semester, but it hadn't been for me. With every class I took, it just felt like I was inching closer and closer to a life I didn't want. So I'd quit, bought a ticket to Australia, and left.

"Not really," she agreed with me. "But dropping out didn't turn out too badly for her. Josie's killing it, and she seems really happy bouncing from place to place." Her eyes took on a faraway look for a moment. "And besides your poor example,"

Amber refocused on me, "she sure seems to think the world of you."

It would have been my turn to blush if I were the blushing type. Which I wasn't. I took a sip of beer and refilled both of our glasses from the jug. "I don't know why she does," I said finally. "But the feeling is totally mutual. If it wasn't for Josie, I wouldn't be back in Canada at all. I tried to get her to come out to see me, but she said she was too busy. Judging by the fact that she isn't even here, I guess that's true. But you didn't answer my question. Are you still in school?"

"Yes and no." She dabbed at her lips with the napkin.

"What does that mean?"

"I was in school," she clarified. "I no longer am. I graduated," she added before I could ask. "In the spring. I just spent the last six months finishing up an internship."

"Congratulations." I raised my glass to toast her. She reluctantly met my cheers. "That's fantastic. So now you're an…"

"Accountant. Pretty exciting, isn't it?"

"Honestly?" I laughed. "Not really. But I know that some people love that kind of thing. You strike me as one of those people who get excited by numbers."

She made a noise halfway between a laugh and a snort. It was oddly sexy. "I would strike you as that type, wouldn't I?"

"Am I wrong?" She sighed, and I got the distinct impression I'd said something very wrong. "I didn't mean anything by it. I'm sorry if I—"

"No. You're not wrong." She interrupted me. "But you're not right, either. I used to love numbers. I loved the idea of looking at them every day and making a career out of it. I mean, they're black and white. Right or wrong. There is no gray or in between. I liked that about accounting. But lately… I'm not so sure. I'm just not really sure anymore that I want to spend the rest of my life being boring and predictable."

Something in her tone told me there was a lot more behind

her words than what she was saying. "And you think that being an accountant would be boring and predictable?" Hell, I knew it was. Just saying it out loud was boring. But obviously, it was a new development for Amber.

"Can I tell you something?" she asked, instead of answering the question.

"Of course."

Amber fiddled with the napkin in her hand for a moment. "I've only just graduated, and I already think I made a mistake." She swallowed hard. "For the last few months, I've busted my ass for my internship. I got there early; I stayed late. I was always available on weekends, and I did everything I could to learn everything I could because I just knew that I wanted the job that I was absolutely sure they'd offer me. It's the most prestigious firm in the country. It would be an amazing career move."

"That's great."

"Is it?" She picked up her glass and drained it.

"Of course it is." I didn't really think so, but I wasn't Amber. And from what I knew of Amber, it seemed as if it would be great.

"Well, they didn't offer me the job when I left," she said. "They said they had a few decisions to make and they'd get back to me."

"Oh."

She nodded and then shrugged. "But I think that might be okay, because I'm not so sure about it anymore."

That took me off guard. "Why not?"

Amber gestured to the jug, so I dutifully filled her empty beer mug. She took another healthy gulp before she answered. "I'm sick of being boring. I'm ready for a little excitement in my life. Something fun and unpredictable." The way she slammed her glass down, as well as the tone of her voice and the way she was looking at me, told me she'd definitely had just enough to drink to be chatty. And maybe to make some poor decisions, too.

As much as I would love for her to make some poor decisions with me, I was way too much of a gentleman for that.

I slid the basket of wings across the table. "You should probably have some more to eat."

AMBER

I KNEW I was drinking too much. I was also talking too much, but I couldn't seem to stop myself. More importantly, I didn't want to stop myself. I wanted to drink, talk, and flirt, and... maybe more.

That idea came out of nowhere. Well, that wasn't entirely true. From the moment I realized it was Cole I'd sat on, my hormones had been in overdrive. Because it was Cole. Something about the man simply oozed sex. From the moment I'd met him years ago, he'd been the unspoken standard I'd always set for sexiness. Unspoken, because there was no way I could ever tell him that I thought he was the sexiest man alive. Never. And I could definitely never tell Josie.

That being said, Cole was the only man I'd ever fantasized about. Ever.

Even when I was with Randy—okay, especially when I was with Randy—it was often Cole I was picturing.

But the only reason I'd let myself fantasize about Cole was that he was safe. Untouchable—a fantasy. Nothing would or could ever happen between us. For one, Cole had been living on the other side of the world. Second, and most importantly, he was my best friend's brother. Which was exactly why there was no way I would ever act on any attraction I might have for him. Not that I actually would, anyway. I didn't do things like that. Never mind the small—yet very important—detail that there was zero point zero zero chance that a man like Cole would ever be interested in a woman like me. We simply were not a match.

I ate two more wings before Cole spoke again. "For the record, I don't think you're boring."

I almost choked. "Yeah, right."

"It's true. I don't."

I shot him a look. If he was trying to tease me, I wasn't in the mood. "Everyone thinks I'm boring. Always have."

Because that's what you've always been.

"Why would they think that?"

I sighed and weighed whether it was worth it to say anything or not. It's not as if we really knew each other, after all. Of course, maybe that made him the perfect person to say something to. "Thing is," I began before I could stop myself. "That's kind of always been my thing."

"Your thing?"

"Boring. Predictable." I shrugged. "When I was in high school, my friends used to call me Mom because I always had things lined up and figured out. Like a walking day planner. It was…still kind of is…the way I am."

"Always?"

I nodded. "Well, not always, but it feels that way." I laughed at myself and shook my head. "At any rate, I'm over it. It's time to shake things up. No more boring."

I expected Cole to laugh along with me, but instead, he just shook his head slowly and lifted his beer to his lips.

"Seriously, Amber," Cole said after a minute. "I mean, maybe you're not the most adventurous, crazy, no-holds-barred woman I've ever met, but you're certainly not boring. Obviously, I didn't know you when you were younger, but would a boring woman agree to stay in a house with her best friend's brother, whom she barely knows, and help him with some renovations?"

I couldn't disagree with that. A predictable woman would never do that. "No, I guess not." I looked down into my drink. "I mean, it's not that—wait." My head jerked up as I realized what he was doing. "What? I didn't agree to help with any renovations."

"You didn't?" He grinned and took a wing from the basket. "I could have sworn you did."

When Cole winked at me, it took all the willpower I had not to melt into a puddle right there under the table. Was it possible that he was flirting with me?

No. There was no way.

I took a moment to compose myself, and then another as I tried to clear my beer-clouded brain enough to formulate a thought. If Cole was really flirting with me, then maybe... no...it was still a bad idea. It was still a no. There was definitely reason number two to deal with. Even if, for some miraculous reason, a guy like him was remotely interested in a woman like me, he was still Josie's brother. But that didn't mean I couldn't have a little fun flirting for a few days. Totally innocent.

And maybe it would be good practice for the new fun version of Amber. I had the rest of my life to be boring and predictable. A few days of flirting would definitely not hurt. Maybe it was the beer, or maybe it was the fact that I was fresh out of a loveless, and super boring, relationship. Or, more likely, it was a combination of everything. Either way, I had nothing more to lose. So I tilted my head and smiled at him. "Maybe I will help with some of the renos." I waited a beat and added, "That is, if you help me with something."

I knew I was playing with fire, but I couldn't stop myself. More than that, I didn't want to, especially when I saw the way his eyes lit up and his nostrils flared with my words. I wasn't the only one having a reaction.

"Oh yeah?" He reached across the table and took my hand. It took everything in me not to self-combust on the spot. "And what's that?"

"I'll help you with the renos…if you take me to the festival." His face fell, and his eyes clouded with confusion. I tried not to laugh as I pulled my hand away and pointed to the poster that hung behind him.

"The First Frost Festival?" He read the poster and turned back to me. "You want me to take you to some small-town festival?"

I nodded and couldn't help the smile that crossed my face. "I do."

He turned around and read some more. "Sleigh rides, an ice castle, and a…" He looked at me. "Frosty Frolic? What exactly is that?"

I shrugged. "I don't really know. But it could be fun. Either way, you don't have to take me to everything. Just a few things."

A sly grin crossed his face. "And do I get to pick which things I take you to?"

I leaned forward and looked him straight in the eye. "I guess that depends on what you pick."

Chapter Four

AMBER

THE SMELL of coffee worked its way into my consciousness, and my eyelids fluttered open. It took me a moment to remember where I was.

Josie's house.

Josie's bed.

Josie's *brother*.

I flipped over to stare at the other side of the bed and instantly wished I hadn't.

It was empty.

I flopped back against the pillow and squeezed my eyes shut in an effort to recover my dreams.

They'd been so real. Cole was lying next to me, kissing me, touching me...

No.

It had been a dream.

Of course, it had been a dream. I wasn't about to sleep

with Cole. No matter how many beers I'd had and how sexy he was and how much I'd flirted with him the night before. And...I had flirted.

My face grew hot with the memory of my tipsy flirting. There was a reason I never behaved that way. I pulled the quilt over my head and groaned.

That was it. I was never drinking again.

Thankfully, it was just my pride that was aching, and I didn't have to deal with any kind of hangover, only a small headache. Nothing a shower couldn't fix. As quietly as I could, so as not to draw any attention to myself, I slipped out of bed and cracked the bedroom door. I peeked down the hallway, but the coast was clear. It was an old house, and I sent up a silent prayer that the floor wouldn't creak as I tiptoed to the bathroom down the hall. It was bad enough having Cole in the house with me; he didn't need to see me in what could only be described as a morning mess, fresh off a very sexy dream about—

"Good morning."

I jumped back as the bathroom door opened. A cloud of steam with a half-naked, still dripping Cole emerged as if I were standing in the middle of a Hollywood romantic comedy. I forgot about my own current state of half-dressed as I stared at him.

If I thought he was sexy fully dressed—and I did—I was absolutely not prepared for the raw sex appeal of Cole Price with only a towel hung low on his hips, inches from me, smelling like soap and...man.

"Amber?"

I nodded, closed my mouth, and tried—fairly unsuccessfully—to pull myself together. "Hi," I managed to say. "I mean...good morning... I mean...I didn't think you'd be...I smelled the coffee and...I was just going to..."

"You were going to shower?"

I nodded again and tried hard not to look at the dip on his hips where the towel hung oh so low. "I didn't think you'd be up here."

His eyes traveled up and down me, no doubt taking in my flannel pajamas and my tossed hair. His lips twitched up into a grin as his eyes finally landed on mine. "I can tell."

My skin exploded in a full body flush, not that he'd be able to tell—I was fully and properly covered up. Still, I tugged at my pajama top and crossed my arms over my chest. Very aware that as covered as I was, I wasn't wearing a bra. "Right. Well, I think I should just…" I moved to walk past him into the bathroom and put an end to the awkward moment. But when he didn't make any motion to get out of the way, I stopped and started again. "Excuse me, Cole."

"Right." His smile was wicked and just a little too dangerous. "I'll be downstairs." He finally stepped forward a little bit, but not enough to let me pass without having to turn to the side and shimmy past him. "We have a busy day ahead of us," Cole added just before I closed the door. "I'll make us some breakfast. I have a feeling we're going to need the energy."

COLE

AS PROMISED, I whipped up a huge breakfast, doing the best I could with the little I found in my sister's cupboards. I was thankful for the distraction, although try as I might, I couldn't get the perfect image of a sleep-tousled Amber out of my head. Even in her perfectly proper, completely typical flannel pajamas, she sparked something deep inside me. Something I would love to explore a little bit more. Just the way I'd love to explore exactly what she was hiding under those pajamas.

Damn that woman.

I forced myself to focus on the breakfast preparations. Amber was the exact opposite of everything I'd ever been attracted to. I preferred my women to be outgoing party animal types, wearing skimpy clothes, throwing themselves at me…always up for a good time. But definitely not a long time.

Maybe it's time for a change?

I shook my head and laughed at myself before I flipped the pancakes. Even if it was time for a change, Amber was definitely not going to be that change. She wasn't the type of girl who did flings. And time for something different or not, I wasn't looking for that kind of different. Not one that tied me somewhere, to someone. That wasn't my style. Besides, Josie would kill me if I messed with Amber. And the last thing I needed to do was piss off the only family member I actually cared about.

No. A little flirting would be fine, but nothing more. I was smart enough to know when to draw the line. Except, when it came to Amber, the line should have been drawn from the moment I laid eyes on her again. Because it was starting to get a little blurry.

"It smells fantastic in here."

I flipped the pancakes onto the plate and turned around to see Amber in the doorway. She was dressed simply in jeans and a T-shirt, with her signature tight blonde braid down her back. It had been nice to see her hair tossed and disheveled from the bed earlier. Something about it made me think instantly about what her hair would look like after spending a night in bed with me. The image filled my brain and sent an electric shot straight to my dick. Damn.

So much for drawing that line.

Somehow, I managed to recover my senses enough to

speak. "It's just a little something I whipped up." I put the plate on the table and retrieved the other dishes from the oven, where I was keeping them warm. "I hope you like your eggs scrambled. I found some bacon in the freezer, too."

"It looks fantastic." She took a seat at the table. "And I'm starving." I poured her a cup of coffee before I sat across from her. "Thanks." She smiled at me and shook her head with a small grin.

"What? Why are you shaking your head?"

"It's nothing." She chuckled a little as she cut a piece of pancake. "I'm just really surprised, is all. You don't seem like the type of guy who cooks breakfast. Or really, cooks at all." She popped the pancake in her mouth, and I had to force myself to look away from her mouth.

It wasn't the first time I'd heard something similar. "Well, I don't know why the kind of men you know don't cook, but I think it's a pretty important skill to have." I laughed. "Besides, working on the ranches in Australia, it kind of becomes a necessity. At least as far as backcountry cooking goes. And it doesn't hurt with the ladies."

"Well, I think it's pretty awesome." She took another bite and closed her eyes as she did so. "This is delicious, Cole. Really."

"I'm glad you like it." It was the truth; I was pleased that she was enjoying it. Despite the fact that Amber seemed to be having a full-body experience with her breakfast, it was refreshing to cook for a woman who actually ate. Most of the women I'd cooked breakfast for just pushed the food around the plate while chugging their coffee. And that was after keeping them up all night. What kind of appetite would Amber have after a night together?

The thought slammed into me, and I was glad I was sitting because there was no way I'd be able to hide the effect she was having on me. Amber was different, that was for sure, even if I couldn't quite put my finger on what made her different. "Eat up," I said in an effort to distract myself from my growing erection. "We have a big day today."

She grinned at me. "Is that right?"

"It is. I spoke to Josie this morning, and she gave me her list of things that need to be done, so we're going to get started with some of the small stuff."

"Like what?" Amber held a piece of bacon poised at her lips.

I tried not to look at her, but it was a losing battle. "The first thing we're going to do is pull up some flooring." It would be hard, dirty work. Nothing sexy about it at all. The perfect distraction. "Are you up for it?"

She chewed her bacon slowly before she shrugged. "Of course. And then later…"

Instantly, my mind raced with the possibilities for later.

"There's a sleigh ride."

It took a moment for me to push aside a dozen or so dirty thoughts that filled my head and catch up with what she was saying. "A what?"

"A sleigh ride," Amber repeated herself. "Although I don't think there's quite enough snow for it. Besides, you did say you'd go to the festival with me, didn't you?"

I laughed. "I did. But I believe I said that I would pick the activities."

Amber put a scoop of scrambled eggs on her plate and shrugged. "Well, just in case you forgot, I thought I'd help you out." She nodded toward my mostly untouched plate of food. "You'd better eat something." She winked. "We have a big day ahead of us."

Chapter Five

AMBER

"I'M SO SORRY, AMBER."

"It's fine, really." I paced the small hallway and examined the faded yellow linoleum. Cole had gone out to the garage to get tools. Whatever tools one requires to pull up flooring. I really had no idea at all. The fact that I'd even agreed to help was almost laughable. No doubt Cole would regret asking me because I had absolutely no experience with such things.

"You're really going to help Cole with the floor?"

"I guess I am." I laughed as I walked to the open door and leaned against the doorjamb, where I could watch Cole in the detached garage. "Maybe I really am full of surprises."

Josie didn't even bother hiding her laughter on the other end of the line. "Right, Amber. I love you. But when I think of you, I do not think of someone full of surprises."

I straightened up and frowned, despite the fact that my friend couldn't see. "You never know," I said. "I just might be." Cole turned at that moment and smiled in my direction, sending my insides into some sort of somersault meltdown.

"Remember, I told you I'm trying something new. I need a change."

"And house renos are where it's at, huh?"

"They might be."

"Whatever." Josie chuckled again. "But do me a favor, okay?"

"What's that?"

"Keep my brother out of trouble while he's there."

My face flushed. "What do you mean?"

"You know my brother. He can be a bit of a…well…" Josie sighed. "I'd really appreciate it if you kept him away from any ladies in town. I'm new, and if I want this house to flip, I really can't afford to make any enemies. It is a small town."

"So you want me to keep him from hooking up with any locals?" I was splitting hairs and completely playing with fire, but I also kind of didn't care. Intellectually, I knew Josie might be pissed if I fooled around with Cole. But then again…she did seem more concerned about Cole getting into trouble with the locals, and as long as I knew what I was getting into…well… there would be no trouble. Besides, no one seemed to believe me that I wanted a little adventure, and maybe Cole being here at the same time was fate's way of lining up just the adventure I needed.

"Exactly," Josie said. "I can't think of anything worse than Cole getting involved with one of the locals."

"I think I can keep him away from the locals." I bit my lower lip while all sorts of dirty thoughts raced through my head. It wasn't a great idea. Getting involved with Josie's big brother was a terrible idea, even if it was for a little no-strings-attached fun. I knew that. I sighed with frustration and walked into the kitchen, where I wouldn't be able to see the subject of our discussion. I'd never be able to go through with it anyway. That was the real problem.

"Are you okay, Amber?"

I nodded before I realized Josie couldn't see me. "I'm fine. Don't worry, I'll keep Cole out of trouble, and we'll get some work done around here. You just take care of whatever it is you need to take care of." I tried to put a smile into my voice. "Don't worry about a thing."

"Thank you." She could hear my friend's relief across the line. "Again, I'm so sorry about not being there. The First Frost Festival in town is supposed to be really fun. You guys really should go to some of the events. Please don't work the whole time—I'll feel terrible."

I picked up the flyer I'd grabbed from the bar the night before. My eyes skimmed the list of events. "Don't worry. I think we'll check out the sleigh ride tonight, although there isn't any snow. This is kind of a strange time for a festival, don't you think?"

"It is," Josie agreed. "When I asked about it in town, it seems that it started almost fifty years ago when the mayor at the time was trying to one-up the neighboring town with their Holiday Festival."

"So by doing it early…"

"Exactly." Josie laughed. "I'm not even going to pretend to understand this small-town stuff. But I do think it's pretty cool."

I nodded. I was starting to agree with my friend. "When are you going to be back? Please tell me it's in time for the big dance on Sunday. There's supposed to be a Snow Ball." I laughed as I said it out loud. But silly name or not, I did like to dance. Some of my best memories of college were when Josie and I would dance the night away at campus parties. It would be a perfect way to end the week.

"That's my plan," Josie said. "I don't want to miss it if I can help it."

"Good. I'm really looking forward to seeing you."

"Me too. It's been way too long." There was a voice in the background, and then Josie said, "Amber? But I have to go now, but don't hesitate to call if you need anything. And thank you again for all your help."

I hung up the phone right as Cole walked through the door. "Was that my sister?"

"It was."

"Did you ask her about the floor?"

I shook my head. "What about it? I thought we were pulling it up."

Cole laughed and handed me some work gloves. "We are. I just wondered how much she wanted us to do. I guess we'll see what we can get through."

"Right." I followed him back to the front foyer and watched while he squatted and turned his attention to the job. I tried to focus on what he was doing, and not on the way his jeans pulled taut against his backside, but it was a battle I was losing —quickly. "We should get to work," I said, more to myself than anything else. I blinked hard and squatted down next to him. With my gloves on, I gripped the edge of the linoleum he'd loosened.

"Okay," Cole said. "On my count, we'll pull up and see what happens. Ready?"

I looked over to see him watching me intently. I couldn't help myself. Something about him made me flirty in a way that was totally unlike anything I'd experienced before. "I've never been more ready." Something flashed in his eyes, and I licked my bottom lip a little before looking away.

Where had that come from?

I had to force myself to stay where I was when all I really wanted to do was jump up and run away. I never behaved that way. Ever!

It took Cole a moment, but he cleared his throat and told me to pull.

Fortunately, once we started working, I didn't have time to think about anything else, except for yanking, pulling, and scraping the old yellow linoleum from the floor. It was harder work than I'd expected, but the time went quickly, and I was surprised that hours had gone by when Cole finally rolled up the last of the old floor and tossed it out into the yard.

"Good work, partner." He wiped the back of his hand along his forehead and leaned up against the wall. Despite the cool weather outside, we'd both worked up a sweat.

"I think we deserve a drink." I draped my arms over my knees, where I sat on the floor, and tipped my head back.

"I think we deserve more than that." Cole crossed the floor until he stood over me.

Despite my exhaustion, my heart sped up by his nearness, and I was thankful we were already overheated so he wouldn't notice the flush that he never failed to bring out in me. I took his outstretched hand and allowed him to pull me up to standing, but he didn't release me right away.

His other hand brushed over my face and moved a stray hair off my forehead. Despite myself, I shivered under his touch. He didn't remove his hand, but instead let it trail down my cheek to rest on my shoulder. For a moment, I was sure he was going to kiss me. And I would have kissed him back, because he was right: we deserved more than a drink. We deserved that kiss, and surely Josie would have to agree.

But then he pulled away, leaving me feeling oddly unsettled on my feet. "We deserve to go on that sleigh ride I promised you."

My mind spun as I tried to process what he'd just said. "The...what?"

He chuckled. "There's no way you forgot already." His smile only made me feel more foolish. "I promised if you helped me out, I'd take you to the festival, remember?"

"Of course I remember. I just thought...never mind." I shook my head and straightened my shoulders in an effort to pull myself together before I made an even bigger fool of myself. I laughed and hoped the sound came out naturally. "We should probably get changed and get moving so we don't miss it."

COLE

AFTER A QUICK SHOWER AND CHANGE, we hopped into my rental truck and headed into town in search of the First Frost Festival. Not that I had any interest at all in a festival of any kind. Sitting on a sleigh, or whatever it was we were going to use, sounded like a certain kind of hell as far as I was concerned. But Amber seemed to be excited by the idea, and for reasons that I still couldn't quite put into words, the prospect of making Amber happy had become more important than anything else.

We stopped at the cafe for a hot chocolate and directions out to the sleigh ride, which was to be held at one of the residents' farms.

"It's at the Stevens' place," the girl behind the counter said when we asked, as if we should know exactly where the Stevens' place was. She gave us a slightly annoyed look and swallowed down a sigh when I asked for directions.

"Thanks for your help." I handed the girl a tip that put a smile on her face and made the annoyance of having to give directions go away completely. "I don't think I've ever been in a town this small," I said to Amber as we made our way back out to the truck. "I thought she might pull a muscle from rolling her eyes when we asked where the Stevens' place was."

"Teenagers." Amber laughed. "But I do think it's cool that there's definitely no fear of strangers here. Everyone seems welcome."

"It's kind of nice." I opened the truck door for Amber and

was rewarded with her beautiful smile. "It reminds me of the friendliness of Australia," I continued when I climbed into the cab of the truck next to her. "I like it."

She smiled again. In fact, Amber was smiling a lot, which was perfectly fine with me. Amber was beautiful when she smiled. Hell, she was beautiful all the time, but when she smiled...there was something particularly sexy about her. Especially because she seemed to just let herself go instead of thinking so much. I got the distinct impression that she spent far too much time thinking about things, and I'd like to know why.

"Here you go, navigator." I handed her the sheet of directions out to the farm and turned onto the gravel road. As it turned out, we didn't need many directions at all. Signs attached to snow-covered hay bales had been set up all over the highway, pointing the way, and soon enough, I pulled the truck into the yard where the festivities were already in full swing.

"Are you ready for this?" Amber eyed me across the cab of the truck with a tilt of her head. She still had her hair in a tight braid, but I hadn't missed the little bit of makeup she'd put on for our—it's not really a date...But I might like it to be a date.

"Am I ready?" I laughed. "You forget I've been living on ranches in the Outback for the last few years. Rides pulled by horses are my favorite way to relax." It was a lie, and we both knew it, but Amber's eyes sparkled as she played along.

"Is that right?"

"In fact, I am the king of hayrides. Never met one I didn't like."

"This is a sleigh ride, not a hayride."

"Are you sure about that?" I raised an eyebrow and tipped my head in the direction of what looked like a large wagon covered in hay bales. "So much for a sleigh, right?"

She shook her head. "I'm not surprised, though. There isn't

enough snow for a sleigh. Either way, it'll be fun. Besides, you're the king of hayrides."

She laughed and slid out of the truck.

I shook my head and joined her outside. I'd done a whole lot more shoveling of hay rather than riding on any. And as far as I was concerned, there wasn't anything fun or romantic about hay, not that it needed to be romantic…after all, we were just friends going out to enjoy the festival.

Still.

"Let's go check it out." I took her hand in mine and started to walk in what looked like the right direction. She stiffened immediately at my touch, and her hand tensed in mine. I looked down at our joined hands before looking up to her pretty face, currently lined with shock. "Oh, Amber. I'm…" I let my thought trail away because I wasn't sorry, and I was definitely not going to apologize for holding her hand when it actually felt like the most natural thing in the world to do. So I didn't. Instead, I winked and squeezed it a little. "I'm excited about this." When she didn't pull away, I tugged gently and led her toward the crowd.

People were everywhere, laughing and talking and just having a great time. Most of them seemed to know one another, which wasn't a surprise, but it became quickly apparent that even those who didn't know anyone—notably Amber and me—would be welcome. We were greeted with handshakes and smiles, and more introductions than either of us could remember. When I explained that my sister was remodeling a house in town, I was handed business cards and pieces of paper with names and numbers for people willing to help with manual labor, pickup trucks, or supplies of all kinds.

It took a few minutes, but finally I managed to extract myself and Amber from the main crowd. I found a small table where I'd been told Moon Juice was being sold.

"What exactly is Moon Juice?" Amber asked the woman

behind the table. She crossed her arms and looked more than a little skeptical about the jars of liquid in front of her. "I mean, I have a feeling that I know what it is, but...do I want to know?"

The woman behind the table laughed good-naturedly. "I'm not sure if you do. Moon Juice is a local specialty, and it definitely has a kick, but I promise you'll love it. We even have a First Frost flavor, iced blueberry."

"That doesn't sound very frosty."

"It's blue." The woman shrugged. "Besides, it's the local favorite."

I couldn't disagree with that, so I handed over the cash, and we each selected a jar before we moved over to where the horses and wagon were pulling up.

"I'm not entirely sure what iced blueberry Moon Juice is supposed to taste like," I said to her. "And seeing how you handled your beer last night, I'm not really sure this is a good idea at all." That wasn't true. I'd loved her flirty little attitude the night before, and I would definitely not complain to see a little more of it.

"Don't be so serious." She swatted at my arm and laughed. "Besides, anything blueberry flavored can't be that bad."

I hopped up on the wagon, turned, and held out my hand to her to assist her up into the stacks of hay. Despite the fact that it wasn't a sleigh, the wagon was strung with pine boughs and wooden snowflakes that had been painted white. Blankets had been strewn around the wagon to protect against the chill that was definitely in the air.

I found us a spot at the back that wasn't very crowded, and we settled down with a red flannel blanket before I turned to her and tugged on her braid. "I think it's more than a little ironic that the woman with her shirt always buttoned right to her neck and a braid as tight as this one is telling me not to be so serious. Don't you?"

She assessed me for a moment, the smile fading off her face before she nodded slowly. "Okay. Fair point."

"You agree?"

"I do." There was no trace of laughter in her voice as she spoke, and for a moment I regretted saying anything at all. I'd been enjoying our light banter. "There's more to me than tight braids and seriousness, you know?"

I tipped my head and examined her. "Is there really?"

"There is. Here." She thrust the jar of Moon Juice at me, and before I could ask what she was up to, she reached around to the back of her head, pulled out the elastic, and unwound her long blonde hair from the confines of the braid. I watched in wonder as Amber threaded her fingers through it and shook out her golden tresses, which resulted in long, wavy locks that were more than a little bit sexy.

I swallowed hard and opened my mouth to speak. But no words came out. I didn't think I'd ever be able to speak again. She was gorgeous. And if I had been attracted to Amber before, I was now completely at her mercy. There was no way I'd be able to stay away from her now.

She flipped her hair upside down and shook it a little before flipping it back over her head and looking at me. "Better?" She challenged me with her eyes, and there was a whole lot more behind that one little word. "I mean, there's not much I can do about the buttons." She gestured to her zippered winter coat that was hiding what I knew was a tightly buttoned blouse. But just the thought of her unbuttoning it had my blood raging hot through my veins and straight to my groin.

Again, I swallowed hard, momentarily rendered useless. After a moment, I regained control of myself and reached out to her. I slid a lock of her hair between two of my fingers, being sure to brush her cheek as I did so. She shivered under my touch, but she definitely wasn't cold. "You're absolutely stunning." If it had been anyone else, I wouldn't have hesitated to slip my hand around her head, cup her cheek, and draw her in for a kiss that showed her exactly how stunning I thought she was.

Hell, that wasn't true at all. If it had been anyone else sitting there with me, I would never have been attracted to her the way I was, because I'd never been so drawn to anyone before. Not. Even. Close.

I let my fingers linger, and for a moment considered going in for that kiss after all. But the horses chose that moment to lurch forward, and the wagon began to move. I pulled my hand back and handed her the jar of Moon Juice that I'd balanced on mine. I tried not to look or read too much into it, but I was fairly sure in the dimming light I saw a flicker of disappointment in her eyes.

Chapter Six

AMBER

HE WAS GOING to kiss me.

But he didn't.

It was for the best.

Or was it?

He was still Josie's brother, after all.

Damn.

I purposely turned away, so I looked out over the edge of the wagon. I took a deep breath, inhaling the crisp evening air, put a smile on my face, and unscrewed the lid of my Moon Juice. I turned and tapped my jar to Cole's. "Cheers. Happy First Frost."

He returned my smile. "This kind of makes us locals, doesn't it?"

"Hardly." I laughed and took a small sip of my drink. Not really sure what to expect, I guarded myself for the harsh burn that I was sure would follow, but the blueberry-flavored alcohol was surprisingly delicious, so I took a bigger swallow. "But maybe this drink makes us locals. This is delicious. Don't you think?"

"Delicious, but...strong." He shook his head sharply.

"Be careful," a man across from them offered. "Mandy's Moon Juice will sneak up on you."

"What is it?" I took another sip. "Because it's delicious."

The man laughed. "No one really knows the recipe, but it definitely is delicious."

"Which is what makes it so dangerous." The woman next to him laughed. "Welcome to town. There's a bonfire down by the river tonight. You two should check it out."

"That sounds fun." Cole looked over at me for confirmation. I nodded. It did sound like fun.

And with the way Cole was looking at me and the warmth of the alcohol in my belly, I was pretty sure I'd say yes to anything he suggested.

"Great," the woman said. "The sleigh ride will take you straight there."

"The sleigh?" I couldn't help but ask. "What's with the hay wagon?"

The woman laughed. "It's always been a wagon. Even when we have lots of snow now. It's just easier, and you can fit more people on it, but the festival organizers insist on calling it a sleigh." Her smile was warm. "I hope you aren't too disappointed?"

"Not at all," I answered honestly and instinctively moved a little closer to Cole.

The woman winked at them and went back to snuggling with her man.

The couple looked cozy and sweet, and a twinge of jealousy hit me. Ever since breaking up with Randy, there'd been more than a few moments where I missed the togetherness that came with being a couple. The companionship that having someone special in your life affords you. Not that Randy and I ever cuddled the way that couple was. In fact, Randy would never have joined me on a hayride, let alone pulled me close in any kind of public display of affection. There'd been a time when I thought that was a good thing. I used to look at couples who hung off each other, held hands or kissed in public, and turned up my nose. They must prove to the world that they're in love, I'd think. It embarrassed me now to remember how judgmental I'd been of that love. But now I knew better. I hadn't been unimpressed with their love; I'd been disappointed in the lack of affection in my own relationship.

The power of the mind was actually a pretty impressive thing. I'd managed to convince myself for years that my love-less relationship was actually the gold standard. I'd been so foolish. But it made sense. At least, according to the last therapist that I'd seen briefly after breaking up with Randy. After hearing about my mother and father's relationship and the way they'd always been so open about their love, even after coming out with the news that my father had a whole other family, it bothered me as a young woman. A lot.

I could never understand how they could behave in such a way that would hurt so many other people. According to Doctor Shultz, I'd begun to think of that outward display of affection, or any real affection at all, as a betrayal.

Of what, I didn't really know. But I couldn't fully disagree with the therapist. That was probably a big part of it. But I couldn't blame all of my issues on my messed-up family life. I knew it wasn't all their fault. It was also my fault. And my choice of partner. Randy just hadn't been right for me.

I didn't mean to, but I couldn't help but watch the young couple and the easy way they leaned into each other. The casual way the man put his hand on her thigh and squeezed. Would I behave that way with the right partner? I sighed deeply and forced myself to turn away. I pulled my gaze back to Cole, who was watching me carefully.

"Hey," he said gently. "What's going on?"

I forced a smile. "What do you mean? We're on a—"

"Where did you go?" He interrupted me. "Just now. You looked like maybe you were lost in your head there for a moment."

I dropped my gaze, but only for a moment before making the decision to be honest with him. "I was just thinking about something I used to have and don't anymore." I took a sip of my drink before wiping my lip and adding, "No, that's not true. I was thinking about something I never had. And thought I did."

"I'm not sure I understand. Why did that make you sad?"

"It didn't." I shook my head gently, enjoying how the waves of my long hair hit my face. It had been so long since I'd worn it down. Years, really. "You know what, it didn't. I just realized that what I thought I had wasn't so great after all. And not at all what I want, or deserve." I looked Cole straight in his eyes. "I'm looking forward to the future, having a little fun and just…well, seeing what happens."

His hand slid across the hay to mine. He didn't take it in his, but I could feel the heat from it, and it sent a thrill racing through me. After a moment, one finger stretched out and wrapped around mine. "Good," he said slowly. "Because I've built a whole life on having fun and seeing what happens and not settling down."

"You don't believe in settling down?" I didn't know why I asked. After all, it's not as though it mattered. Not really.

He shrugged. "I guess I haven't thought about it much. But I definitely don't believe in labels."

"Labels?"

He laughed. "When you label things, they tend to lose their fun. Don't you think?"

I could lose myself in his eyes and his words, but only moments before I let myself fall, I caught myself. "But there's more to life than just having fun, isn't there?"

He chuckled. "Spoken like a true accountant."

"Maybe." I ignored the twinge of hurt I felt at his words. Boring. Predictable. "But I think I'm starting to see that it should be a balance. I'm twenty-four," I said. "And more and more I'm thinking that there's no reason that you can't have both. Fun and responsibility."

He nodded slowly. "Have you ever had any? Fun, I mean?"

My first instinct was to clap back with a sharp retort. Of course, I'd had fun. Tons of it. But...had I? Really? After a moment, I took a breath and answered honestly, "Not enough. Growing up, our family was kind of a mess. It's a long story, really, but basically my dad had two families. Finally, he left his first family for us, but then it was messy, with a lot of hurt feelings, and...well, I didn't want to make any waves. I thought that if I could just be the good girl, then my older brothers would like me instead of blaming me for breaking up their family."

"Wow."

I nodded. "Yup. It was a lot of wow."

"So you didn't do anything rebellious?"

I laughed. "That was my little sister, Chelsea's, job. I never did any of that wild and crazy stuff you're supposed to do when you're a teenager."

I hadn't intended to get into my family life with Cole. It was never easy to explain to people that my younger sister and I were the products of a long-running affair, and when our father finally left his other family to be with us, it had basically destroyed the lives of all six kids. I'd mostly come to peace with the situation, but there was no denying that the choices of my parents had shaped who I was.

As if he could sense that I didn't want to get into any more details, Cole squeezed my finger with his and smiled. "Well, it's never too late. We both have some Moon Juice, and we're at a festival in a town where no one knows us. I can't think of a better time to have a little of that wild fun, can you?"

"No." I laughed. Maybe it was the Moon Juice, or the night sky, or sitting next to Cole, or a combination of everything, but in that moment, I had never felt more free. "I can't." They each raised their jars and drank deeply. In the back of my head, I knew it was a bad idea to let loose completely, but the part of me that no longer cared was a lot louder than the part that did. I took another drink right as an eerie howl split the peaceful night. I jumped up, and my drink splashed over the edge as I scooted closer to Cole on the wagon.

"What was that?"

Cole chuckled and wrapped an arm around my shoulders, pulling me close as if it were the most natural thing in the world. "I imagine it was just a coyote in the distance. Don't be scared."

I wasn't. At least, I wasn't scared of any faraway coyotes. No, if I was scared of anything at all, it was the way my stomach fluttered and my body burned at Cole's touch. That was downright terrifying.

COLE

I LIKED my arm around Amber. I liked it a lot.

So much so that I didn't bother moving it until the wagon arrived at the river and the bonfire. I helped her down from the wagon and once more took her hand in mine. It felt natural. As if it belonged there.

Everything about spending time with Amber felt natural. Even though I definitely wasn't interested in rushing into anything, I couldn't help but think that despite what I'd said earlier about being the type of guy who had lived his whole life without being serious, maybe I could be. Serious. At least when it came to a girl like Amber.

The fire was roaring and it looked as if the entire town gathered around the flames. The two of us slipped into the crowd, chatting and laughing with the locals easily, as if we'd always lived there. The entire time we mingled, I was very much aware of Amber's presence next to me. Every time I looked at her, my attraction spiked a little more. With her golden hair framing her face and bouncing in loose waves over her shoulders, and the way her smile lit up her face in the fire-light every time she laughed, she was completely mesmerizing.

Finally, I was done making small talk and listening to stories about Crystal Creek. Maybe it was the Moon Juice I'd had, or the beautiful woman by my side, but I was more than ready for something a bit quieter.

We'd been separated by some of the locals, and Amber was talking to a group of women when I slid up behind her. I smiled as charmingly as I could at the women and bent to whisper into her ear. "Come with me for a minute. I need to steal you." I had to physically hold myself back from nibbling on the creamy skin of her neck. As it was, I inhaled her scent deeply and it definitely wasn't the alcohol that had me off-balance. Without waiting for an answer, I took her hand and with a quick apology to the women, pulled her away from the crowd.

"Where are we going?"

"I just don't want to share you anymore." I winked at her. "Besides, we should enjoy this fire a little bit, don't you think?"

She nodded and squeezed my hand tighter as I led her through the crowd. The bonfire was huge, with most of the party gathered on one side. But as we circled the fire, it was clear that the opposite side was going to be much more private. Piles of hay bales stacked high created seating both near the fire and a little farther away, toward the mostly frozen river. I found a quiet spot and climbed up on the hay into a private nook where we were both close enough to the fire to keep warm and far enough away that we weren't likely to be interrupted.

"You don't want to share me?" Amber asked once we were settled into the hay. She leaned in toward me.

It may have been the Moon Juice, which definitely was more potent than I'd expected, but she'd been flirting with me all night. It was subtle, but she was definitely flirting. A fact I didn't mind at all.

"Are you having fun?" I answered her question with another one.

"I really am." She nodded. "Thank you for bringing me."

"A deal is a deal." I reached over and took her hand, slipping my fingers between hers. "Besides, I've really enjoyed myself with you tonight. A lot."

I couldn't be sure in the dim light, but I was fairly sure she blushed. The idea of her skin flushing because of me turned me on. With my spare hand, I reached up and stroked her soft hair. "You look beautiful tonight."

There were so many reasons I shouldn't do it, but the reasons that I should outweighed any objection I could think of. Before I could let myself be talked out of it, I leaned in and pressed my lips to hers.

She tasted like blueberry and something even sweeter. Something that was all Amber. Her lips yielded to mine and I deepened the kiss, cupping her cheek with my hand to hold her to me. A small moan escaped her lips, sending a spark through me directly to my core. I pulled her tight, needing her closer still.

It was clear that one taste wouldn't be enough. I deepened the kiss. My tongue traced the seam of her lips until she opened to me. And when our tongues twined together, I was sure it was the most erotic thing I'd ever experienced. I pressed her back into the hay, settling into the kiss.

I could have kissed her all night. Only it didn't take me long to realize that when it came to Amber, I was definitely not going to be satisfied with only a kiss.

Reluctantly, I pulled away and sat back to look at her. Her eyes were still closed, her lips parted and moist, but only for a second before she realized I was gone. She brought her fingers to her lips and opened her eyes.

"What?" She shook her head slightly. "Why…why did you stop?"

"I just thought that maybe I—"

"Oh." Amber's hands fluttered in front of her face as she sat up. "Of course." She turned away slightly and smoothed her hair back off her face. "You're right…we shouldn't… okay…" She nodded. "I get it. You're not…I'm not really…"

"What?" I shook my head in confusion over what exactly was going on with her. I couldn't help it and I laughed a little, which only seemed to fluster her more. "What are you talking about, Amber? What's going on?"

"This…you…me…" She took a breath and attempted to compose herself. "I get it," she said after a moment, finally turning to look at me again. "This is silly. We shouldn't do this and I'm not really your type and we probably—"

There was no way I was going to let her finish that thought. I moved quickly and in an instant I straddled her body with my legs, so she couldn't move. A second later, I took her face in both my hands and kissed her deeply and thoroughly. When I was done, there was zero room for doubt about whether or not she was my type.

When I was finally sure I'd made my point, and Amber's chest was heaving, her breath coming in short pants, I pulled my mouth away but didn't make any move to leave her personal space. With the firelight dancing over her face, I looked directly into her eyes so she could see that I meant every word of what I was about to say. "Don't ever doubt that you're my type, Amber. I can honestly say with one hundred percent accuracy that I've never wanted any woman the way I want you right now. Not. Even. Close."

Her lips turned up into a sexy smile, but she still didn't look convinced. "Then why did you stop?"

"Because I just thought that maybe—"

"Josie." Her face fell. "Of course." She shook her head. "Your sister. I'm a terrible friend."

"Stop." I held her face so she was looking at me again. "I didn't stop because of Josie. In fact, I can tell you that when I was kissing you, my sister was the very last thing I was thinking of."

"But I mean, you're her brother."

I nodded.

"And I'm her best friend."

I nodded again.

"And—"

"I don't see how one has anything to do with the other."

Her eyes squeezed closed for a second. "I promised her I would keep you away from the local women."

I laughed and swung my leg over her so I sat next to her again. "I think you did a pretty good job of that, don't you?"

It took her a moment, and then she joined my laughter. "I guess I did."

"She didn't say anything about you staying away from me, did she?"

Amber shook her head.

"Good." I twisted my fingers in her soft hair and pulled her gently toward me. This time, instead of tasting her sweet lips, I moved to her neck.

"But I think that maybe—oh..."

I trailed kisses down her skin, biting and licking my way down her neck.

"Maybe she meant that I should—ohhh..."

I got to the zipper of her jacket, which I moved easily down and out of the way so I could ease the buttons of her blouse from their holes until finally, my lips had access to the deliciously tantalizing swell of her breasts. I continued and deftly unfastened the next button, exposing her cotton bra.

"I just don't know if we—oh, that feels good." She shuddered under my touch, encouraging me.

Her breasts fit in my hand perfectly. I couldn't wait to see them properly. But that would have to wait. For the moment, I'd settle for teasing her to the point of distraction. I nibbled my way along the top of her bra before I pushed it down to expose her pebbled nipple. My body reacted to her sharp intake of breath as I swirled my tongue around the peak before I popped it into my mouth and sucked gently.

"Do you think that Josie—"

"Okay." I sat up. The last thing I wanted to do was leave her beautiful, perfectly pink nipple, but I couldn't listen to one more second of her talking about Josie. "We can either talk about my sister," I said pointedly. "Or we can do this." I raised my eyebrows and tilted my head. "But we can't do both."

I waited for her to answer, but I didn't have to wait long because a second later, Amber reached up, wrapped her arms around my neck, and pulled me down to her.

Chapter Seven

AMBER

IT SEEMED AS THOUGH it took forever for us to get back to the little house after the bonfire. Not that I was complaining. Because with every minute that passed before we could get home to Josie's little house and into a proper bed, my desire built until finally I thought I might explode with my need for the man whose kisses sent me into a spiral and whose touches lit a fire in me that I didn't even know existed.

Finally, the wagon returned us to the farm and Cole's truck. A short drive later, we were at the front door, and I was fiddling with the lock. The entire time, Cole hadn't stopped touching me.

"Don't tell me you locked it?" He wrapped his arms around me and held me tight as I tried to manipulate the lock.

"Of course I did. It's..." I stopped myself. Maybe locking the house was safe, but what I was about to do with Cole was decidedly not. And I loved it.

Finally, I managed to turn the key and open the door. I barely had a chance to step inside before Cole had spun me around and pushed me up against the wall. He twisted his fingers in my hair and tipped my head back to expose my neck. My knees buckled beneath his attentions.

"I've been wanting to do this all night." He nibbled and licked and finally pulled back to unzip my jacket and tug it off my shoulders.

Earlier, after he'd unbuttoned my blouse, I'd left it, even after zipping up my jacket to ward against the cold November air. It was so simple, but it made me feel daring and a little sexy and risqué just having my blouse undone, my breasts exposed in such a way.

But as sexy as I had felt earlier, it was nothing compared to the way I felt as Cole finished unbuttoning my blouse. The hungry look in his eyes as he exposed my bare flesh to him sparked a hunger of my own in me.

Had I ever been wanted in such a way?

Not even close.

Nor had I wanted a man the way I wanted Cole.

I had just enough Moon Juice in my system to allow myself to shut off that annoying little voice that earlier had tried to talk me out of doing exactly what I was about to do. But I was plenty sober, and as Cole leaned forward and pressed his lips to my skin, I was glad I was because if this was going to be a one-time thing, I planned to remember every single second of it.

A low moan escaped my lips as Cole continued kissing me. First the swell of each breast, then between them, until his mouth traveled down my stomach and to the waistband of my jeans.

His fingers made short work of the button before slipping beneath the denim to cup my cotton-clad bottom. I stiffened, and a shiver ran through me.

Was he going to…

"Amber?" He must have sensed my hesitation. Still on his knees, he looked up at me, a question in his eyes. "Do you want me to—"

"No!" I yelled the word and immediately clamped a hand over my mouth. He laughed, and I couldn't help but join him. "I mean," I tried again. "No. If you were going to ask me if you wanted me to stop. The answer is no." It's definitely a no.

"You seem a little..."

I shook my head and bit my bottom lip a little, annoyed at myself for stopping him when it had been feeling oh so good.

"I'm fine," I said. "Honestly. I've just never..."

His eyes flashed with desire, and a slow smile crossed his handsome face. "You've never?"

"I mean, I have. Of course." It had never occurred to me that my sexual inexperience would be an issue. And it wasn't as if Cole and I hadn't had sex. Wait—I needed to correct that. It wasn't as if Randy and I hadn't had sex. Of course, we had. It was just...boring. Dammit, I hated that word! I swallowed hard. I might as well get it all out there. "I've just never done, well..."

"This." He lifted one eyebrow mischievously and, in one quick movement, shoved my jeans down over my hips into a puddle at my feet. A second later, his hands still on my ass to hold me in place, he leaned forward and, using his teeth, he tugged on the elastic of my panties.

A shiver ran through me. Damn, I was in trouble.

His hands moved around my waist. Two fingers slipped under the waist of my panties, but before he did anything more, Cole looked up and met my eyes with an unasked question. I nodded in response, and it was all he needed to push my panties out of the way, too, leaving me fully and completely exposed in front of him.

Instead of being embarrassed, the way I thought I might, his reaction only emboldened me. I took a few steps and freed myself from both my boots and my clothing so I could spread my legs to keep from falling over.

Not that I would, with the grip Cole had on my hips. He made a noise that could only be described as a growl before pulling me to him and kissing me between my legs.

COLE

SHE WAS ABSOLUTELY DELICIOUS. Everything about her. But when I pressed my mouth between her legs to taste the sweet juices there, I was completely lost. I forced myself to move slowly, taking my time with her. I'd guessed she was probably not that experienced in the bedroom, but even so, I may have underestimated how much she'd been missing out on.

I planned to rectify that.

At once.

With my hands gripping each of her thighs, opening her to me, I used my tongue. Slowly at first, and then, as she began to respond to me, faster. She was so responsive, so completely trusting of me, and willing to let go. It was sexy as hell.

But not nearly as sexy as when she threaded her fingers in my hair and pressed me into her with an unspoken request for more. A request I was more than happy to deliver on.

I focused my attentions on her swollen nub, sucking gently before swirling my tongue in circles. I could feel her tense beneath my grip as her orgasm neared. I knew I'd be the first to make her climax this way, and I was determined to make it memorable. Keeping one hand firmly gripping her hip, I used my other to slip first one finger and then another inside her.

She gasped as I pressed into her tight heat. Before her legs gave out, she wrapped them tightly around me and groaned as I hit the sensitive spot deep inside her. I pressed her up against the wall to keep her from sliding and at the same time took her throbbing clit into my mouth. Seconds later, she came completely undone around me, screaming out her release as her climax overtook her.

I smiled as I finally pulled away. I hadn't expected her to be a screamer, but then again, Amber was full of surprises.

And I liked it.

A lot.

Reluctantly, I got to my feet because, as much fun as I was having, I was still completely dressed, including my winter coat, and things were definitely starting to heat up.

I took a moment to watch her as she recovered from her orgasm. Her eyes were squeezed tight, her palms pressed flat against the wall, and her chest rose and fell with her breasts straining against the innocent cotton bra she still wore as her breath began to slow. I knew now, despite the innocent cotton undergarments, she was anything but. And I liked it.

"You are without a doubt the sexiest woman I have ever met." The sound of my voice caused her to open her eyes, a blush instantly covering her skin. Before she could move to cover herself, a situation I definitely did not want, I reached out and cupped her cheek, letting my thumb trace her lips. "I mean it, Amber. Damn, woman."

Her lips flicked up a little into a grin. "That was…" She shook her head, unable to form the words.

"Incredible?"

Amber nodded. "Very."

"I'm glad." I pressed my thumb between her lips, and she sucked it before biting it ever so slightly, a move that made my cock stiffen. A painful reminder that I was still fully clothed.

And not anywhere near done with her yet.

I stripped my jacket and boots off, leaving them scattered in the hallway before leading her to the couch.

"You still have far too many clothes on."

I grinned. "I do, don't I?"

"Let me help." Amber reached out and tugged my T-shirt up and off my head. She ran her hands down my chest, sending thrills through me, directly to my core. Her fingers slowly worked the buttons on my jeans, and after what felt like forever, she got them undone and slid the denim over my hips, along with my boxer briefs.

Her eyes widened appreciatively as my jeans hit the floor, a detail I definitely noticed and liked very much. But not nearly as much as when she wrapped her hand around me and squeezed before walking back toward the couch. She reached behind her back and unclasped her bra, releasing her gorgeous tits.

As much as I wanted the evening to go on forever, I had my limits, too. And I'd just about reached them.

After a quick dig through my wallet for a condom, I sheathed myself and joined her on the couch. There were probably more romantic places, but it didn't matter. The only thing that mattered was being inside her, feeling her around me, and looking into her eyes.

Her blonde hair was splayed out on the cushion beneath her, making her look every bit the sex goddess I was quickly coming to believe she was. But she was also so much more. She was Amber.

I looked straight into her eyes as I sank deep inside her. I saw the want in her eyes, the need...and something else that both sent a thrill through me and scared the hell out of me at the same time.

Chapter Eight

COLE

I SLEPT REMARKABLY BETTER with Amber in my arms than I had the night before on the lumpy couch with her a flight of stairs away. A lot better. And it didn't have anything to do with the location of my slumber.

I didn't want our night to end. After our lovemaking session on the couch, we'd moved upstairs, where Amber fell asleep with her head on my chest. I'd never been the type to linger after a hookup. And I most certainly wasn't the type to spend the night cuddling. But with Amber, it was different. I was different. It was the craziest thing, but the more and more time I spent with her, the more time I wanted to spend with her. She was definitely more than a hookup.

She was…

Waking up.

Next to me, Amber stirred a little, and a sweet sound, almost like a sigh, escaped her lips.

The sun was starting to peek through the old blinds that covered the window. If I had to guess, it was probably just after seven. Too early. The night wasn't long enough for me to soak in every bit of having her body pressed into mine. The silkiness of her hair splayed over my chest. The gentle inhale and exhale of her breath as she dreamed.

I snuggled Amber closer to me and kissed her bare shoulder. She mumbled in her sleep and wiggled a little into me. I tightened my grip and stroked my hand down her bare arm. "Good morning," I whispered in her ear.

Amber turned in my arms and looked up at me. She really was the most beautiful woman I'd ever seen. The very fact that I was thinking that way should scare the hell out of me, but it didn't. In fact, it was exactly the opposite. With Amber, in only a few days, I felt oddly settled in a way I had never felt before. She actually had me thinking things I'd never thought before… relationship things. And that was the scary part. Because I knew it couldn't last. A thought I didn't feel like exploring yet.

It took her a moment to wake up completely. She blinked her eyes a few times and finally offered me a tentative smile. "Hi."

I kissed her softly. "Hi, yourself. Did you sleep okay?"

She nodded, but the peace I was feeling wasn't reflected in her eyes, and I knew exactly what the reason was. Morning-after regret. But I'd be damned if I let her feel even a moment of regret for what had happened between us.

"Don't do that."

"Do what?" She blinked hard and shook her head.

"Don't feel bad about…well, anything. Because I don't. And if I remember correctly, you enjoyed yourself, too."

She blushed, but it was followed by a laugh. "I did." She took a moment before she added, "And I don't regret…well, that."

"Good." I kissed her quickly.

"But it's not just that."

I was a little slow on the uptake, but I put the connection together about what she really felt bad about. Relief that it wasn't me she regretted washed through me, but only for a second. "No," I said with a shake of my head. "Amber, please don't worry about Josie, okay?"

"I'm not." She tried to turn away, but I caught her face.

"You're a terrible liar."

"I know. It's just…"

I waited, and when she didn't finish her thought, I offered a solution. "We don't have to tell her."

"What?" She scooted back to the other side of the bed.

"Just hear me out," I said quickly. "It's not like we planned it to happen. She'll be here tomorrow, and the reality is, I'll be going back to Australia soon, and you'll be…"

"Getting a job."

"Right. You're going to get that kick-ass job offer in Toronto's most prestigious and exciting accounting firm." I didn't mean to sound sarcastic, but it definitely came out that way. "At any rate, technically, I don't think you're breaking any kind of friend code or anything. But since you're worried about it, maybe we just shouldn't tell her?"

Amber pulled the sheet up higher on her body, a fact I really didn't appreciate because Amber's body was something that should never be covered up, and eyed me warily for a moment. "I guess you're right," she said finally. "I mean, it's not like this is going to actually be anything more than a little festival fun anyway."

Her words hit me in the gut despite the fact that she was right—that's all it would ever be—but hearing her say it out loud took me off guard, and her words stung. Not that I was going to say anything about it.

I watched as a smile slowly crossed over her face. The sheet slipped a little, revealing just enough of her creamy white breast to make my body stand up and take notice. And when, instead of reaching to pull it back up, Amber crooked a finger and beckoned me toward her, it was all the invitation I needed.

AMBER

AFTER A VERY LATE SLEEP-IN–NOT that we actually did much sleeping—I fixed us both a quick breakfast of instant oatmeal and coffee so we could get some work done on the house. I didn't say anything, but I was definitely feeling like helping Josie out was the very least I could do for her after… well…after Cole. It didn't matter what he said about it; I couldn't help but feel guilty about sleeping with my best friend's brother.

On one hand, I knew my friend would be excited for me that I'd finally let loose long enough to have a little fun. And man, did I ever have fun. Just thinking about the way Cole made me feel with a few kisses and touches on my body was enough to make my body vibrate with need again. I'd had a few lovers before, if you could count one fumbling high school hookup and Randy's thirty seconds of moves—which I didn't —but I'd never experienced anything even close to what I'd experienced with Cole.

Of course, leave it to Miss Plan Everything Out Perfectly to finally let myself relax enough to have my first wild fling with my best friend's brother. I could have blamed it on the Moon Juice, except that even though the drink was strong, I was completely sober the night before. And this morning. Not only that, I very much wanted all of it to happen.

I snuck a glance at Cole across the table, where he was finishing his coffee.

Oh yes, I'd very much wanted that to happen. And I wasn't going to lie—there wouldn't be any complaining from me if it happened again. None whatsoever. The future could be dammed because living in the moment felt damn good.

I could hardly believe my own thoughts and how far I'd come in such a short time. I liked it. A lot.

"So what are we going to do today?" Cole gathered our dishes from the table and piled them in the sink.

"I thought you said something about pulling all the base-boards and moldings off?" I sipped my coffee and looked at him in confusion. "You're running this show," I added. "At least until Josie gets back."

Cole laughed. "I meant, what First Frost Festival events are we going to attend today?"

"Festival?"

He crossed the floor and kissed my forehead sweetly. It was such an intimate and unexpected gesture; something flipped in my tummy. Just temporary, I reminded myself. He'd said so himself. He was going back to Australia, and I was going to take a super boring job at a super boring accounting firm and go back to leading a super boring life in a big city where I was just another face in the crowd. It didn't matter whether I was trying something new by trying to break out of my mold a little. It was only temporary. I was destined to be boring and predictable.

And even if that was true—which it was—there was no reason that I shouldn't have a little fun while I could. Because that's all this thing between us was. Fun.

"Did you still want to go to the festival?"

"A deal's a deal, Amber. Of course I want to go." He returned to the sink and ran water over our dishes. "What's going on today?"

I smiled and quickly ducked my head so he couldn't see how much it pleased me that he wanted to go, but I was too slow, and he turned around and caught the grin on my face.

"What?" Cole grabbed a tea towel to dry his hands. "What's that look for?"

"Nothing."

He moved quickly, crossed the room in two steps, pulled me up from the chair, and kissed me. Hard. I couldn't stop the way my body responded immediately to his kiss. "Tell me," he said. "What are we doing today?"

My stomach flipped, and my whole body quaked with desire just from being in his arms. I took a deep breath. "You have two choices."

"If either of them involves spending time with you, I don't care either way."

Again, my stomach danced. "Are you sure?" I liked playing with him because as soon as he heard the choices, I was fairly positive I knew what he was going to pick.

He looked straight into my eyes and spoke with such an intensity that for a split second, I forgot that what we were doing was temporary. "I've never been so sure of anything, Amber."

I swallowed hard and worked to keep my composure. "Okay. Two choices. We can go to a Polar Bears versus Arctic Foxes paintball fight this afternoon and do the baseboards later."

"Or?"

I grinned because I was absolutely positive he'd like the second option the best. "We can take care of the work around here first and then go for a drink tasting at the Tipping Cow."

"That's the bar we went to the other night?"

I nodded. "And after that…there's a thing called a Frosty Frolic. I'm not really sure—"

"Sold." He kissed my neck and moved up to my earlobe,

where he whispered, "If it involves you and frolicking, I'm absolutely in."

"I thought so." I laughed and, as much as I didn't want to, wiggled out of his grasp. "Then we'd better get to work."

After a little bit of convincing and the promise that I would finish up the dishes, Cole reluctantly left me to get started on the baseboards. He seemed much more motivated to get the work done with the promise of some frolicking. I was still chuckling at the look on his face when I'd presented the options to him when my cell phone rang. Assuming it would be Josie, I picked it up without looking at it. "Tell me you're on your way."

"Well, since I have no idea where you are, that would be pretty hard."

"Declan!" I shrieked into the phone. I hadn't heard my half-brother's voice in months. Way too long, as far as I was concerned. I'd been so busy finishing school, and up until the last few months, my brother's activities with his nonprofit foundation had him in some third-world country, making things better for those who were less fortunate. We just hadn't had time to connect.

"Hey, little sis."

"Just because I'm twelve months younger than you does not mean I'm your little sister."

Declan laughed. "That's exactly what it means." The fact that we were half-siblings and our father had been living two lives at once, with two separate families, hadn't been an issue between us since we were kids.

I ignored him. "I miss you. Are you still in Cedar Springs?"

"I can't imagine being anywhere else." I could hear the love in his voice. "Of course, there's been a few trips back and forth, but Cedar Springs is definitely home now."

I still had a hard time wrapping my head around all of my siblings being in Cedar Springs. Together. Never in a million years would I have thought that we'd all be able to put our feelings aside and be a happy family after everything that had happened with our parents. Especially Ian and Mitch, my oldest brothers. They'd taken their father's betrayal the hardest and, for many years, had refused to have any relationship with Chelsea and me at all. That had changed recently, but I still hadn't met Ian and Mitch, at least not properly.

When I didn't say anything right away, Declan added, "You're surprised, aren't you?"

"Yes." I laughed. He knew me too well. "Not that you're in love—that's fantastic. But I never would have guessed that you would settle down in a small town. But if that's where your heart is…"

"It is," Declan said quickly. "So much. And I can't wait for you to meet Evie. She's amazing."

I had heard all about my brother's new fiancée, as well as Ian's new fiancée, and of course, my movie star brother, Cal's, new love. And then there was Mitch, who'd taken it to a whole new level and fallen in love, gotten married, and gotten pregnant in record time. Hell, I'd barely met Mitch, and now I had a whole other family to meet, and I was going to be an auntie. At least Chelsea wasn't getting married. Yet. But after the last time I'd spoken to her, it seemed as if even my little sister had also found love in the small mountain town.

I risked a glance down the hall, where I could hear Cole starting to get to work. Maybe I'd found love in the prairies?

As soon as the thought settled, I pushed it out. Temporary. One night and one morning of hot sex—very hot sex—wasn't love. Far from it.

Even if my heart was starting to think so.

"When are you coming?"

"What?" It took me a moment to realize Declan was asking me a question. "Coming where?"

"To Cedar Springs, silly. The lake…to come visit and meet everyone properly. A lot has changed with everyone."

Reflexively, I shook my head, even though my brother couldn't see me.

"I hear Christmas here is beautiful," Declan continued. "And with Jonah, Evie's little guy, it's going to be so fun. Amber, you have to come."

"Oh, I don't know."

I did know, and the answer was—no.

Chelsea had tried to get me to go visit Cedar Springs, the tiny lake town in the middle of the Canadian Rockies, to see our half-brothers a few months earlier. At the time, I'd used the excuse of having to finish up my internship, which wasn't totally an excuse. But the truth was, I also wasn't in a hurry to visit my two older half-brothers for the first time. There were four brothers altogether. But Chelsea and I only had a good relationship with the two youngest, Declan and Cal. Likely because when the scandal of our parents blew up, we were all young enough to be forgiving, and when we ended up in school together, a friendship formed. That wasn't the case with the older ones, Ian and Mitch. Chelsea had met them both over the summer and swore to me that they were great guys. But despite everyone's attempts, I just hadn't been able to get in the one big happy family mood. Maybe that could change, too?

"I don't think so," I told Declan. "I'm kind of busy."

"Is that right? Didn't you graduate a few months ago?"

"I did."

"And Chelsea said you were finishing up an internship and you haven't accepted a job yet. So the way I see it—"

"I'm not going." I could only deal with so many things at once. "Not this time, Dec."

"Okay." His voice was kind. My brother knew when not to push. He was genuinely one of the nicest people I'd ever met, which was exactly why he was in the perfect profession. "So tell me," he shifted gears, "what are you up to these days? You're done with school, you haven't taken a job yet...and...that's totally unlike you. Are you feeling okay?"

I laughed and walked through the kitchen, out the back door, and into the crisp November morning air. There was the distinct smell of snow lingering in the air. Maybe we'd get a big snowfall after all. A lot of things were going on that were totally out of character for me, I thought, thinking of Cole. Declan didn't know the half of it. "I'm taking a bit of a break to figure things out. I'm just feeling a little unsure of everything right now."

Where had that come from? I wasn't taking a break. Not really, anyway...

"That doesn't sound like you at all."

"That's the point." It felt good to say it out loud. "I think I'm more than ready for a change. I'm not the same little girl anymore who needs to control everything."

"You're not?"

He knew he was teasing, but I was serious. Even I hadn't been fully convinced that I would be able to let go of my need for control, but the last few days had proved otherwise.

"Do you want to talk about it?"

I laughed.

"What? I'm a good listener," Declan protested.

"I know you are. And yes, I'd like to talk about it, but I really don't know what more to say. I'm in the middle of Saskatchewan right now."

"Saskatchewan?"

"Right? I know, it's crazy. My best friend Josie is flipping a house in this tiny town in the middle of nowhere, so I came for a little visit. After that, I don't know. A few days ago, I would have said that I'd take a job and start my life as an accountant."

"But now?"

"Now I don't really know." It was a truthful answer, but it

hurt my heart a little to say it out loud. "I mean, I guess I do know," I added quickly. "I will take a job at some point, but I'm just being silly because I know that's what I'm going to do, but they didn't offer me the job the way I thought they would."

"They still might."

He was right, and I knew it. "They might. In fact, I really do think they will." I took a deep breath. "But when they didn't, it kind of threw me for a loop, and I got to thinking that maybe there was more."

"More?"

I shrugged. "Like what you have." I hadn't even realized until that moment that my brother did have a lot of what I was looking for. "You travel and do new things. You don't have every minute planned out. You just kind of...live."

"Amber." There was so much kindness and love in his voice that it made me even more emotional. "You know there isn't one right way to live, right? You're not doing it wrong."

"I know, I know," I said the words, but as I did, I shook my head as if I didn't fully believe them. "I just had this crazy idea that maybe I could...I don't know."

"What? What do you want to do?"

"That's just it." The emotion built until finally I felt like crying. I never cried. "I don't even know, Dec. I just know I don't want to be boring anymore."

"Oh, Amber, you're not boring. You're fantastic." There was nothing disingenuous about what he said; I knew he thought the world of me, but it still didn't feel like enough.

"You have to say that because you're my brother." I walked across the grass, enjoying the crunch of the thin layer of snow we did have under my shoes. I inhaled deeply, wrapped my sweater tighter, and tried to let the peacefulness of the morning wash through me.

"That's not true. I get to say whatever I want because I'm your brother." He laughed again, and this time the sound made me want to hug him. "So I'm going to say this," he continued. "You aren't boring. I would never think that of you. But I do know that even the most exciting people sometimes feel like they're in a rut. So if you're feeling stuck, for whatever reason, shake it up. Your life is totally up to you, Amber. You can be and do anything you want to do. It's your life. So live it the way you want."

"You make it sound so easy." I turned back towards the house and caught a glimpse of Cole through the window.

"It really is. I promise you," he said. "You might think that there's a lot weighing on what you decide to do, but mostly we build things up in our heads. And really, the world will not collapse if you decide to do something different from what you originally planned. If you don't want to take an accounting job right now, don't. Maybe it is time for you to try something new. Go travel, see the world. Meet new people. Do something that makes your heart sing. We have one life. It doesn't have to be hard."

"Are you sure?"

"I've never been more sure, Amber. Honestly. We're allowed to change our minds. Whenever we want."

Change our minds.

Live life the way you want?

Could it really be as easy as Declan seemed to think it was?

On the other end of the line, I heard someone calling for Declan. There was some mumbling, and then my brother came back on the line. "Amber, I gotta go. But I'm serious... this is your life. Follow your heart."

"Okay."

"Promise?"

I laughed. "I promise, big brother."

COLE

I WATCHED Amber on the phone. Whoever she was talking to, it wasn't my sister. I knew that because she'd just texted me to let me know she'd be there early the next morning, and not only was she looking forward to seeing us both, but also going to the Snow Ball. I hadn't even thought about the ball. Of course, I also had barely given any thought to Josie coming home.

Hell, the only thing I'd been able to think of was Amber. It hadn't even been forty-eight hours since she'd sat on me on the couch, yet the woman had somehow managed to consume every single one of my waking thoughts since. And my sleeping ones, too. Those ones were really good.

But not nearly as good as they'd been in reality. She was something else, that was for sure. Logically, I knew that whatever was going on between us could never be more than a fling —how could it be? We were going in different directions, doing different things with our lives. Even if it did make me think of trying new things. New relationship things.

That was a thought I never expected to have. Ever. But Amber was changing the way I thought about a lot of things. Or maybe it was just that I was changing and she'd come along at the right time. Or maybe…it was a little bit of both?

"How's it going in here?"

I hadn't noticed Amber come inside. I'd been so lost in my thoughts about her. It took me a moment, but I swallowed hard and cleared my throat.

"They'll go a lot faster with you here."

She laughed and picked up a hammer. "Then let's get moving. We have some frolicking to get to."

There was no way she could know how her words affected me, but damn.

I took her hammer away and smoothly replaced it with a crowbar. "You can start over there. Try not to break the boards when you take them off. We'll reuse whatever we can. Assuming Josie wants to reuse them, that is."

We started working, and I did my best to keep myself focused on the job. After all, she was right: the faster we finished, the faster we could get to the fun part of the day. Never mind the fact that the organized Frosty Frolic event wasn't until midnight. I was pretty sure I could create my own event right there at the house without much prompting at all.

"Tell me about Australia." Amber pried one end of a baseboard off, resulting in the satisfying give of the old nails.

"What do you want to know?"

"Why Australia?"

I laughed. I get that question a lot. Mostly from my parents when I first moved. "Honestly?" She nodded and turned to listen to the answer. "Because it was as far away as I could get at the time," I said matter-of-factly. Of course, I'd given my parents a very different answer. Something about loving the movie Crocodile Dundee when I was a kid, and always wanting to see the Outback. But to Amber, I gave the truth. "If I'd have stayed at home, I would have ended up like my dad, and I couldn't think of anything worse than that."

"Doesn't your dad own a hardware store?"

"He does. He wanted me to get a degree in business and run it with him."

Amber tugged on the piece of trim she was working on, and it came off in her hand. "Why was that so bad?"

"It's not, really." I shrugged. I'd thought about it a lot, how unfair I'd been to my parents. "But you know when you're young, and you think you know everything."

She laughed. "I guess."

"Well, maybe you weren't so cocky. But I was very dramatic, and I was so sure that if I did what they wanted me to do, I'd miss out on something."

She turned to look at me. "I've met your parents. They seem really nice and happy enough."

"They are. And I suppose it wouldn't have been so bad if that's all I wanted out of life. But I wanted more than just nice and happy enough, you know?"

"I do." Amber's face creased into a frown, and she nodded. "Well, I guess I don't really know. But it doesn't seem so bad, I guess."

I laughed, but there wasn't much humor there. "It seemed absolutely horrible to me at the time." I shook my head and continued. "It still does in a way. I think there's just so much more out there. I didn't want to settle for happy enough. I want to be ecstatically happy."

"I don't think that's real life." She waved the crowbar slightly. "I mean, don't you think ecstasy is an unrealistic expectation?"

I couldn't help myself. I grinned wickedly and wiggled my eyebrows. "Not at all."

She blushed and waved me away. "Okay, okay. But besides that. Seriously," she said. "Don't you think it's unrealistic to expect every day to be extra?"

"No." I didn't even have to think about it. I shook my head. "I don't. I don't think anyone should ever settle. Life should be an adventure, with excitement at every turn. It should be fun. I mean, it's your life."

"I think that seems nice, but it's just not reality."

"Why not? We only get so many trips around the sun," I argued. "Why not make the best of them?"

Her face changed, and I caught the shadowed look of defeat in her eyes before she shrugged and turned away.

"You don't agree?" I softened my voice, put down my tools,

and crossed the room to her. Earlier, I'd tried to tell myself that I could keep my hands off her for the day, at least until we got our work done, but suddenly that seemed like a terrible idea. I wrapped my arms around her and dropped a kiss on her neck.

Amber turned in my arms. "What was that for?"

"You seemed a little bummed, and I don't want to see you sad. Especially if it was something I said."

She forced a smile that was clearly fake, but it was also clear that she didn't want to talk about whatever had bothered her. "I'm fine. Let's get this finished and go see what's happening with the festival today."

I kissed her gently. She might not want to talk about it now, but I was pretty sure it was a subject I'd be revisiting with her. Especially considering I hadn't even told her how I really felt. That my feelings were changing every day. I wasn't ready to admit it yet, but more and more, I couldn't help but think that I would trade my life of excitement at every turn for the love of a woman. A woman like Amber.

No, I really wasn't ready to admit that out loud yet.

So instead, I smiled broadly. "Deal." For now, it was definitely easier to play my cards close to my chest. No sense getting ahead of myself.

Chapter Nine

AMBER

I ALMOST FELT guilty for the lack of work we'd done on Josie's house. On one hand, we had made a little progress, and it was fair to say that we'd done some things. But there was no doubt that if Cole had been visiting his sister on his own without me to distract him, he could have accomplished at least double the amount of work.

On the other hand, I was enjoying my time with Cole so much that I really couldn't feel guilty about it. Besides, it was coming to an end soon. Josie would be home in less than twenty-four hours, and our little…whatever it was would come to a crashing halt.

I snuck a glance in Cole's direction as he navigated the truck towards town. Freshly showered, he smelled even more amazing than he usually did, and I needed to sit on my hands in the truck to keep from grabbing him and kissing him. Then we'd never get to the activities in town. And despite the attraction of staying in with Cole, I'd really enjoyed the first night of the festival and was excited for more fun.

"What did you say was happening at the Tipping Cow?" Cole asked when he saw me looking at him.

"I think it's some sort of drink tasting," I answered. "Some of the locals create a unique cocktail, and there's a vote at the end of the night to see which one was the favorite. I think there are a few other things going on in the main square, too. Besides, it will just be fun to walk around and take it all in."

"You like the small-town stuff."

It wasn't a question, and I didn't bother denying it anyway. It was true. I'd grown up in a suburb of Vancouver, and although it definitely wasn't the big city, it was far from a small town. After graduation, I went to school on the other side of the country in Toronto, which was as opposite from a small town as you could get. I never thought of myself as a small-town girl. Maybe it wasn't something I could sustain for a long time, but there was no doubt that seeing a town with such a close sense of family was appealing. Really appealing.

Maybe moving is an option after all?

There were still so many questions about my future. And now that I'd opened my mind to the possibilities of actually having a choice instead of taking the job at the firm if it was ever offered, there suddenly seemed to be even more options than I'd ever considered.

"I really do," I finally agreed with Cole. "I've just never experienced this type of thing before. It's kind of cool."

"It is. But you know, you don't have to live in a small town to experience that."

"I actually think that's the whole point."

"No. You don't." He pulled the truck into a space against the curb, turned off the ignition, and looked at me. "Working at the ranch over in Australia is just like that. I mean, it's definitely not a small town, but it's bigger than a family. The best way to describe it is like a community. There are a lot of things going on, and everyone cares about one another. It's actually pretty fantastic." Cole hopped out of the truck and ran around to help me down from my side.

"It sounds pretty good," I said truthfully. "So I assume you'll go back."

"To the ranch? No."

"Why not?" I stared at him, but he only shrugged in response. "I mean, if it's as great as you say it is, why wouldn't you want to go back?"

"There are lots of places in the world," Cole answered easily. "Why settle for just one?" He took my hand in his, and we walked towards the main square, where people were gathered. Children ran around while the parents stood around various fire pits, sipping hot chocolate and apple cider. The whole scene was incredibly small-town, and it made me happy just to watch it.

Cole made it sound so simple, and I couldn't help but envy his easygoing attitude. He was right. There were a lot of nice places in the world, and I'd love to see some of them. I'd never been the type of person who had wanderlust in my veins, but then again, maybe I could be. Maybe I'd just done a really good job of burying it beneath all the responsibility I thought I had. Maybe it was something else to consider.

"The drink tasting is in here."

We stood in front of the pub, and Cole laughed. "Was it the sign Snowflake Spirits and Brr Brew that gave it away? Come on, let's go check it out. I think I could definitely use some Brr Brew. What about you?"

"I think I'm more of a Snowflake Spirit kind of girl."

I laughed, and once again I found myself relaxing in his presence. It was so easy to be with Cole. Something about him just made me feel comfortable.

We walked in and found seats at the bar. Cole was served

something that was blue and smelled faintly like black licorice, while my drink had some sort of smoke coming out of the clear liquid with a glass rimmed in sugar.

"Cheers." We toasted our frosty concoctions and drank them down. They were better than we expected, and for the next round, we switched and ordered what the other was having. I drank my second drink much more slowly, fully aware that in the last few days I'd had more alcohol than I'd probably had in the last six months combined. I wanted to ask Cole about what would happen when Josie got home, but I wasn't sure how to bring it up. Would we continue our...whatever it was? Or would it end as quickly as it had begun? I could have made myself crazy thinking about it, and the last thing I wanted to do was ruin our evening, so in the end, I just said what I was thinking.

"So, Josie will be home tomorrow."

Cole nodded. "That's what her text said. Oh, and she asked me to get some costumes for tomorrow night's party."

"Costumes?" I groaned. "I hate costumes. Besides, Halloween was last month. Why costumes?"

"It started years ago," the bartender interrupted with a shrug. "Sorry," he added. "I couldn't help but overhear you."

"It's okay," I said. "But tell me, why costumes? I thought it was the Snow Ball?"

"About ten years ago, there was a terrible virus that spread through town right before Halloween. Most of the kids were too sick to go trick-or-treating, so they kind of postponed Halloween. Since it was so close to the First Frost Festival, the mayor just decided to combine the celebrations into one. It was a tradition that just kind of stuck. It's fun."

"Costumes are fun," Cole agreed. "But where will we find something on such short notice?"

"I know just the place." He handed Cole a piece of paper with a phone number on it. "Katie will hook you up. She brought in a truck full of options so the people who weren't able to leave town to go to the city to get something would have a few choices. I'm sure she'll have something left. Give her a call."

"Thanks, man." Cole smiled mischievously, grabbed the paper, and tucked it into his pocket.

"Well, aren't you going to call?" I wasn't sure whether I should trust the look in his eye.

"I am."

"But?"

"Do you trust me?"

I laughed in response.

"Wait here." Cole stood. "I'll be right back. Stay right here."

I DID as he asked and watched him leave the bar to make the call. I kind of wanted to know what the costumes would be, but at the same time, I didn't much care. I had never been a big fan of costumes. If it had been up to me, I wouldn't have dressed up at all. But if Cole was excited enough to sort them out, I'd be happy enough to go along with it.

"Another drink?" The bartender held up my empty glass. "I can make you a Spiked Icicle or a Frosty Freeze if you want to try something new?"

I laughed because he managed to say the names with a straight face. "I'm not sure I want to know what a Spiked Icicle is."

"It's really good, I promise. I'll get you one of those."

I shrugged, but didn't bother protesting. It's not as though I had anything else to do. Besides, I was having fun, and I definitely couldn't remember the last time I'd had such a good time.

As if the universe had some kind of limitation on how much fun I should be having, my cell phone rang. When I glanced at the number on the screen, my heart leapt into my throat. Joshua Magnus, my internship supervisor from the accounting firm in Toronto.

I should let it go to voicemail. I was, after all, sitting in a bar, drinking themed drinks on a Saturday afternoon. I wasn't drunk by any stretch of the imagination, but was I in any state to talk to Joshua?

Probably not.

But I couldn't *not* answer it. It just wasn't my style.

My heart raced. Maybe it was the alcohol I'd consumed, but probably not, that made my hands shake as I took a deep breath, pressed the button, and put the phone to my ear.

"Mr. Magnus, hi." I put my business voice on and hoped I sounded more professional than I felt.

"Oh, I'm glad I got you, Amber. I was half expecting to get your voicemail. It is Saturday after all, and sometimes I forget that not everyone works as much as I do. Some people actually have a life outside of work." He chuckled, but his comments hit me in the gut. I was one of those people. "But what am I thinking? I'm talking to you."

I flinched. But he was exactly right. The entire time I worked at the firm, I hadn't once accepted an invite to join my coworkers for a drink after hours or shared in the stories of what I'd done over the weekend. In fact, it only took a few weeks until no one bothered to ask me what I'd done over the weekend. I'd worked. Everyone knew that.

With the very notable exception of the last few days, I'd pretty much done nothing interesting for the last few years unless it involved school or the internship, and that wasn't all that interesting. "Right," I said after a moment. "And why are you working today, Mr. Magnus?" I knew why he was calling. It could only be for one reason. The job. I was either going to be offered the position or be told I wasn't the right fit. My stomach roiled, but not because I was afraid of not getting the offer. Just the opposite.

Things had changed a lot in the last few days. Maybe there were other options after all? I glanced out the window, where Cole was speaking into his phone.

The full-time position at the firm might not be the only thing on the table anymore.

But if it was offered...would I be able to say no? Had I really changed that much?

"As you know, Amber." My attention was drawn back to the conversation. "We've been considering all the interns for the full-time position as junior analyst." I nodded despite the fact that he couldn't see me. "And your resume, along with your work experience with us, is very strong."

"Thank you."

"Right, well, besides your impressive credentials, I must tell you, Amber, that I have been particularly impressed with your work ethic while you were with us. You remind me of a younger version of myself. You work hard, you make the right sacrifices to get ahead, and you get the job done. I can always count on the quality of your work, and I know that if I need anything, you're not just a clock puncher. No matter what it takes, I know you'll make the firm a priority. Your first priority."

I was conflicted by his words. On one hand, it was the highest praise I could have received from him; yet, on the other, listening to him describe me made me sad. Would I really sacrifice anything for the firm? Would I truly make it my life? At the expense of everything else?

My stomach churned because deep down, I knew the answer. I would. It's who I was. It was how I was wired. Maybe I was destined to be boring and predictable forever. To settle down in a predictable job and live a predictable life doing predictable things.

Was that really such a bad thing?

"And because of all of those qualities, Ms. McCormick," he continued. "It's my pleasure to offer you the position as the newest junior analyst here at Wallace and McKwade Financial Services."

I'd expected it, of course—despite trying to talk myself out of it—but hearing him say the words out loud sent a thrill through me. Followed by a shot of icy terror. I pushed my empty glass away.

The job was everything I'd ever wanted. Everything I'd ever worked for. And it was happening. I should be excited. Over the moon. I should be… "Really?"

"Absolutely," he said. "You deserve it. Now, you don't have to give me an answer right now. In fact, I would—"

"Oh no," I said before I realized what I was doing. "It's a fantastic opportunity, Mr. Magnus. I'm happy to…" I let the thought trail off. I'd been ready to accept the position. But something stopped me from saying it aloud. I glanced out the window and saw Cole, who still stood outside talking on his cell phone.

It was ridiculous not to accept a job because of a man I was having a casual relationship with. It was downright insane.

"Decisive. I like it." Mr. Magnus was talking. It took me a moment to catch up and realize that he'd misunderstood what I'd said—or not really finished saying. "I'm very happy to hear it, Amber. You will be an excellent addition to our team."

"Oh, Mr. Magnus, I—"

"Call me Joshua." He chuckled. "You're one of us now. You start on the thirteenth. I trust that gives you enough time to prepare yourself."

"It does, but—"

"If you have any more questions, I'm sure the team in HR

will be able to help you out. But if not, I expect to see you bright and early on the thirteenth, Amber." He laughed again, a sound that was starting to give me a headache. "What am I saying? I'm talking to you. I'm sure you'll be the first one in the office."

Before I could protest again, or even process what had happened, the line went dead, and the call was disconnected.

In a daze, I reached for the new drink that the bartender had placed in front of me while I was on the phone.

I'd just been offered everything I'd ever wanted. And it seemed that maybe I'd accepted it, too. I should be thrilled. I should be celebrating. Instead, I sat numbly and stared at the smooth countertop.

"Hey," Cole said a moment later when he returned to the bar. "Are you okay?" He squeezed my shoulders and brushed his lips next to my ear in a way that made my stomach flip with the familiarity of the action. He sat next to me and put his hand on mine. "You look a little...I don't know. Off."

That was putting it mildly.

I wanted to tell him what had just happened. And more importantly, how conflicted it had made me feel. And maybe if it had been a real relationship, I would have. But it wasn't. So instead of saying what I was feeling, I once again swallowed down my feelings and forced a smile to my face. "It's these drinks," I lied. "I think they're hitting me. But I'm okay now."

He looked at me as if he were prepared to challenge me further, but then his cocky grin returned. "There's that smile," he said. "Must be because I'm back."

I shook my head with a laugh. I liked that about him. He made me laugh. Really laugh. "Must be."

He signaled the bartender for a new drink and turned back to me. "Seriously." His voice changed. It was softer. He was genuinely asking. "Are you sure you're okay? You can talk to me, you know?"

I wanted to. So badly that it was almost a physical ache inside me. What was this man doing to me? In a matter of only a few days, I'd gone from knowing exactly what I wanted out of life to being completely and totally confused. And there was no way I could tell him any of that. And I especially couldn't tell him that, even though what we were doing was just supposed to be fun and no strings, I was starting to have feelings. Real ones. No. I definitely couldn't tell him that.

Besides, in a few days, he'd be gone, I'd go to Toronto to start the new job, and we'd never see each other again. "I'm good," I lied. "I'm looking forward to the frolic later." That wasn't a lie.

Cole leaned forward and kissed me on the lips. The openness of our relationship, or whatever it was that we were doing, took me off guard a little bit, but I liked it. A lot.

"I'm looking forward to it, too." He kissed me again. "Really looking forward to it."

Chapter Ten

COLE

I COULDN'T SHAKE the feeling that something was bothering Amber, but I wasn't going to push either. She'd talk to me if she were ready. But maybe I'd been wrong, and there really wasn't anything wrong. After all, she was smiling now. I glanced over at the beautiful blonde, whose smile only made her more radiant.

I'd never been one to question happiness, and there was no reason for that to change. So for the time being, I was going to take the smiley, happy, beautiful woman on my arm and enjoy the rest of what the day had to offer. And I was pretty sure that was a whole lot.

We finished our drinks at the Tipping Cow and, needing some fresh air, ventured out into the town square. I had never been one for the quaintness of a small town, but something about Crystal Creek was getting to me. I glanced at Amber, who held my hand as if we were a real couple. I wasn't even going to pretend that it wasn't Amber's influence that was making me feel so good. I knew damn well it had everything to do with her.

We strolled towards the focal point of the square. The gazebo was decorated with giant wooden snowflakes that had been painted light blue and white and dipped in glitter, and pine bough swags that hung along the banister. I couldn't help but want the walk to last longer. Heck, I wanted everything with Amber to last longer. Knowing that Josie was coming home and would crash our little arrangement was bittersweet. Of course, I wanted to see my little sister, but I desperately wanted to spend more time with Amber.

"What?" She caught me staring at her. She blushed a little and tucked a stray hair behind her ear.

"I was just thinking how beautiful you were."

She blushed harder, and the sexy pink flush that worked its way across her creamy skin was totally worth the lie, which wasn't really a lie at all.

"Let's sit."

"I have a better idea." Amber tugged on my hand and started to walk in the opposite direction. "Let's check out the ice castle."

I laughed. "It's not dark enough. Let's wait."

"No way. Besides, it's not like it's a haunted house."

"It is kind of crazy, isn't it?" I asked. "This whole Halloween, winter festival mash-up?"

"I like it." She grinned. "Besides, I really don't think the ice castle is meant to be haunted or creepy, but if it is, dusk is the best time to check it out."

"I think you're crazy, but okay." I shrugged and laughed again because ultimately I didn't care what we did, as long as I was with Amber. The thought hit me out of left field. I'd literally only been in a relationship…or whatever it was…for forty-eight hours, and already I was thinking about how I never wanted her out of my sight. And that's what was crazy. But surprisingly, I wasn't scared. And I definitely didn't want to run away. Maybe I was really growing up? The thought made me want to laugh. My whole adult life, I had made it a point not to settle down, not to get attached. Maybe that was changing? No, it was definitely changing. Fast.

The ice castle turned out to be an excellent idea, especially because Amber clutched tightly to me at every turn. It really was a mixture of a winter wonderland with frosty features in the form of glitter and a few spooky Halloween holdovers. Occasionally, something would jump out or fall on us, and whenever that happened, Amber worked her way a little closer to me. But that wasn't even the best part.

Just as we were navigating our way through a room that had been designed to look like a giant igloo, a polar bear jumped out and grabbed at Amber's arm. She shrieked, and I spun her so she was sheltered in my arms and nuzzled under my chin. As I turned, I caught sight of the staircase and got an idea. When Amber had gotten up to go to the bathroom, the bartender in the Tipping Cow told me a little more about the ice castle and that it was a little bit famous for couples to sneak upstairs and fool around in one of the upstairs rooms. I hadn't planned it, but since the opportunity presented itself…

Without saying a word, I took her hand and led Amber up the stairs and away from the chaos below.

"Where are we going?"

"Just to take a little break." I found the first door and tried the handle. It was locked. I tried not to laugh and tried the next one. It opened. I popped my head around the corner and checked. The room was empty. Perfect.

"What are we doing?"

Conveniently, there were candles and a book of matches lying on an old dresser. I lit them, illuminating the dim room. There wasn't much to it, except a few chairs and an old sofa. I pulled my jacket off and laid it on the sofa for her to sit on. She giggled at my chivalry and sat.

"I wanted to talk to you is all." I finally answered her as I sat next to her.

"You couldn't wait until after we were done?"

I took her hand and shook my head. "I really don't think I could. Besides, any excuse to get you up here and alone." I held her face in my hands and kissed her thoroughly. I couldn't get enough of her lips, and the more I kissed her, the more I wanted to. I'd kissed a lot of girls, but none like Amber.

"Well, I can't argue with that." She touched a finger to her lips when I pulled away. "I can't believe the weekend is almost over. I mean, I know we still have all day tomorrow, and I wasn't planning on leaving until Monday morning."

Her words hit me in the gut. Leaving? I didn't even want to think about it.

"And Josie will be here tomorrow morning." Amber was still talking. "I'm excited to see her, but…"

"But you're kind of enjoying the way things are?"

She nodded. "Is that silly? I mean, I know it is. We're not… I mean, this isn't…we're just having fun."

I ignored the implication of her words. "We are having fun. But I was thinking." The idea hit me like a flash. There really was nothing to lose, so I took a deep breath and said what I was thinking before I could change my mind. "There's no reason that we can't continue… this."

"This?" Amber sat back and looked at me as if I'd just told her I was really a Tibetan monk. "What do you mean?"

I took a breath and silently reprimanded myself for being nervous. I was never nervous around women. Besides, it's not as if I were asking her to marry me. I was being ridiculous. "All

I'm saying is, we've been having a lot of fun together. And I like you, Amber."

"I like you, too."

That made me happier than I expected. I grinned. "And life is too short not to have fun. Don't you agree?" She narrowed her eyes in question. Maybe that had been the wrong choice of words. Dammit. Why was it so hard for me to say how I really felt? "So why don't we keep the good times going?"

I had to force myself not to groan out loud. That was definitely not the right choice of words.

"Keep the good times going?" She shook her head. "What does that even mean?"

I ignored the warning bells ringing in my head and pushed on with my idea. Maybe if I just got the words out properly, it would all make sense. "What it means is that I think you should come with me when I go back."

"Go back?"

"To Australia." I grabbed her hands and squeezed. "Life is way too short not to make the most of it. And you said yourself that you didn't have any immediate plans now that you've graduated, and the job wasn't offered to you right away, so why not? Let's go see the world and have a little fun. Together."

AMBER

TOGETHER?

See the world?

My mind raced. What was he saying? Was he drunk?

Did he seriously think he could sit here and ask me so casually to drop everything and go with him to the other side of the world? Sure, we'd been having fun, but that was different. It was safe here. It wasn't Australia. Besides, we were temporary. We were only having a little fun—no attachments. We were not the get serious—move to the other side of the world—change your life completely—kind of together.

Were we?

I blinked hard, trying desperately to process his words. But I couldn't think straight. I'd been offered my dream job. And now...I was being offered...something so much different.

Could it be a different dream? Could I really let go of my plan to take a chance?

He was squeezing my hands in his and watching me intently for the answer that no doubt he expected to be a big hell yes. I could see it in his eyes. He wanted me to jump up and say yes without a second thought. And dammit if I didn't want to do just that.

But I couldn't.

It just wasn't who I was, and despite how much I wished I could be someone else, do something else, it just wasn't me.

Was it?

"Amber?"

The smile on Cole's face morphed into a look of concern and maybe even a little irritation because I hadn't answered him. But what did he expect? He couldn't seriously expect me to be excited about this. The very fact that he'd asked the question was giving me heart palpitations.

"Say something, Amber." He moved one of his hands and smoothed back a stray hair from my cheek that kept escaping my braid. "Anything. Just say something."

"What the hell are you thinking?" It wasn't exactly the best choice of words, and certainly I could have thought of something better to say, but the words slipped out before I could think of anything else.

Cole recoiled and sat back. "What was I thinking? I was thinking that we like each other and we're having fun and—"

"Fun? We're having fun," I repeated, making the word fun sound like something very, very bad, which in that moment, in that particular context, it really felt like. "Do you really think I could drop my whole life for a little fun?"

Cole released my hands and crossed his arms over his chest. "Why not? There's nothing wrong with enjoying life, Amber."

"I am enjoying it."

"Are you?" His eyes flared. "Because it seems to me that until I came along, you were merely existing. Tell me I'm wrong."

I jumped up and paced across the small room. How dare he!

My stomach hurt. My heart raced. I wanted to cry and scream all at the same time. It wasn't at all how I'd planned the night to go.

Because you did plan it. Just like you plan everything, Amber. Because you're boring. Predictable and boring.

I forced the voice in my head to be quiet. I took a fortifying breath and turned around. "I can't." The edge slipped from my voice as I answered him. "I can't tell you that."

He stood, but didn't make a move towards me. "Then come with me." His eyes pleaded with me. "Just come."

"It's not that easy, Cole."

"It really is."

"I got the job." The words fell from my mouth and burned my tongue on the way out. It was an amazing opportunity at a prestigious firm. It was exactly what I wanted; I should have been thrilled.

I should have been. But I wasn't. And wasn't that exactly why I hadn't told Cole about it earlier?

I knew it was.

Everything I'd been pretending at for the last few days with Cole was just that—pretend. As much as I would like to think otherwise, I was who I was. It had been determined a long time ago. I was boring. Destined to live a life of predictability.

And really, was that such a bad thing?

"The job?" He took a step towards me. "You got it?"

I nodded and hugged my arms around my body. "They called earlier. They offered me the job."

"And you took it?"

I shrugged.

"You did, or you didn't."

I looked down at my feet for a moment. "I guess I did." I knew that wasn't entirely true. Sure, Mr. Magnus had misunderstood me earlier, but that didn't mean I had to sign up for a life I didn't want.

I could say no. I could turn it down. I didn't have to go for the safe choice. My whole life, I'd taken the safe route, the path of least resistance, where I would be safe, where I would know exactly what would happen next.

I didn't have to do that now. Not if it wasn't what I really wanted.

I looked up at Cole. Everything we'd shared together for the last few days flashed through my mind. It had been fun, spontaneous, and, truthfully, some of the best days of my life.

But it was scary.

I squeezed my eyes shut and looked down again.

Maybe it was too scary.

"So you're going to be an accountant?"

"I am an accountant." I jerked my head up and swallowed hard to keep the tears at bay. I would not cry. Not like this.

"I guess congratulations are in order."

His words bit into my skin like acid. I hadn't really expected him to be happy for me. I hadn't expected much from him, really. But I hadn't expected him to be hurtful.

"So you're going to give it all up for some boring job?"

"Give what up?" The room was suddenly a lot colder than it had been a moment ago, and I wrapped my arms tighter around me. "What exactly would I be giving up, Cole? This is all I've ever wanted."

"Is it?"

I swallowed hard and nodded.

"I don't believe that."

I opened my mouth to defend myself, but he still hadn't answered my question. "What am I giving up, Cole?"

"Everything." He shook his head and rubbed his hands over his face. "You're giving everything up, Amber. You just spent the last few days telling me how you weren't sure what you wanted to do with your life, but what you did know was that you needed a change. I just offered you a change. I just offered fun and adventure and…"

"And what?" I forced myself to keep my eyes open when all I really wanted to do was squeeze them shut and will him to say the words that I didn't even realize I wanted to hear until that exact moment. "What else did you offer me?"

He opened his mouth and closed it again. "It doesn't matter. Sounds like you already made your choice."

Choice? What was he talking about? I'd taken a job. That was the right thing to do. I'd been ridiculous to even think there might be any other thing to do. I was a college graduate, and I needed a job. That was what you did. You graduated and got a job. Besides, he hadn't offered me anything else, except fun.

What had I wanted him to offer?

The answer to that question scared me more than it should have. Because I knew exactly what I'd wanted him to say—that he had feelings for me—because didn't I have some for him?

It was all too much.

Anger grew inside me. I was supposed to be happy about

the job. I was supposed to be excited about my future. I was getting everything I'd planned for.

Even if you no longer know if you even want a plan?

I shook my head hard in an effort to make the stupid voice in my head shut up once and for all.

"There was no choice," I said after a moment. The words came out soft and hurt, and it pissed me off because I didn't want to feel any of those things when talking to Cole.

"There was." He crossed the room and stood only inches from me. Despite the flood of mixed feelings flowing through me, a shiver of desire rippled through my body. His voice was cold, tinged with disappointment and hurt. "There still is." He looked at me with so much intensity that maybe I didn't need him to voice anything out loud after all. Maybe he was saying everything I needed to hear with his eyes?

I opened my mouth to change my mind. To tell him that I'd go. That I didn't want the job at all. That what I really wanted was—him.

But before I could say anything, Cole spoke again. "I'm sure you'll be very happy with your boring, predictable, planned-out life. After all, it's all you've always wanted."

His words pierced through me and lodged painfully in my heart. To hear him so coldly express his opinion of me hurt more than I could have ever expected.

Standing in front of him, the man I never would have expected to have any feelings for beyond simple lust, especially after such a short time, I had two choices. I could break down and cry. I could admit out loud for the first time that he was right, and that I was terrified that I was making a mistake, that I was going to regret taking the safe road and not risking everything, but that I was just too scared to do anything else.

Or…I could go with the safe choice, the way I always had: protect my heart and my future.

I swallowed hard and squeezed my eyes shut, but just for a

moment. When I opened them, I looked Cole right in the eye and made my choice.

"Screw you, Cole Price." Before I could stop myself, my hand flew out and slapped him across the cheek. The sound of it hurt more than the sting in my palm, but not nearly as much as it hurt to turn around and leave him standing there.

Chapter Eleven

AMBER

THE NIGHT BEFORE, after storming out of the ice castle and making the short walk in the cold November night back to Josie's house, I half expected Cole to be waiting for me. I wasn't sure whether I was relieved that his truck wasn't in the driveway or disappointed. After going inside, making myself a peanut butter sandwich, and taking a hot shower to warm up, he still wasn't back, and I'd given up hope that he would walk through the door and apologize.

Did he even need to apologize? Should I be the one to say sorry? After all, I'd hit him. The questions rolled through my head on a continual loop all night. I'd lain awake in Josie's bed, staring at the ceiling and trying to make sense of what had happened in the ice castle. What had Cole been saying before I'd gotten mad? And why had I gotten so upset?

I at least knew the answer to that one. I was upset because he'd called me out. And he had no right to do that.

Or did he?

Maybe he had a point. Maybe I shouldn't have taken the job. Maybe I was choosing a safe, boring path for my life. But what was my other option? I didn't have any. I'd made a choice a long time ago, whether I realized it or not, that the only way to be sure that your life wasn't going to self-implode was to keep close tabs on it, and make sure every detail was planned. Period. Besides, it wasn't as if Cole were offering any real alternatives.

Or was he?

Even if he had been serious about going to Australia, what we had together was only two days of fun and recklessness. That wasn't enough to base any major life decisions on. I was smarter than that. I was safer than that.

With so much rolling through my head, it was a surprise that I'd been able to get any sleep at all. My alarm went off at seven the next morning, and I woke disoriented, groggy, and shocked that I'd managed even a few hours. The urge to pull the covers over my head and ignore the outside world was strong. But Josie would be home in less than an hour after catching an early flight, and ignoring my best friend was never an option.

I would definitely need coffee to get through the day. And lots of it. Before I left the room, I took my time dressing in jeans and a clean sweater. I tied my hair in a braid so tight it hurt. Cole liked my hair down. More the reason to keep it pulled back. That way, if he was downstairs…what? I couldn't even finish the thought. Part of me wished with every fiber in me that he would be sitting at the table with a fresh pot of coffee, waiting to talk to me, but the logical part of me knew he wouldn't be.

Sure enough, by the time I pulled together enough courage to go downstairs, I walked into an empty kitchen. There was no sign of him anywhere. More than that, there was no indication that he'd even come home the night before.

Where would he go?

He didn't know anyone else in Crystal Creek, and I hadn't noticed any motels. Even if there was one, it was likely all booked up because of the festival.

Should I be worried about him?

No. A man like Cole, so full of adventure...he'd be fine.

"He probably found someone to go to the Frosty Frolic with after all." I spat out the words and instantly wished the idea hadn't popped into my head. I knew Cole wasn't a monk, but the idea of him with anyone else hurt me in a way that I'd never felt before.

Sick to my stomach, I managed to prepare a pot of coffee and a meager breakfast of toast that I only picked at. I didn't realize how long I'd been sitting at the table, staring into my half-empty coffee mug, until the front door opened.

I flinched, splashing coffee all over the table and my sweater.

"Cole?"

The second his name was out of my mouth, I regretted it. No way did I need him to think that I'd been sitting around waiting for him.

"It's me." Josie's voice rang out.

Josie? Shit. Of course.

I quickly swiped my hands over my hair and pushed up from the table to meet my friend. "Josie. Hey."

"Hey, yourself." She pulled me into a hug and squeezed tight.

I wrapped my arms around my friend and bit the inside of my cheek to keep from crying the unexpected tears that threatened.

When she pulled away, I took a good look at my friend. She looked the same. Only better, and I told her so. "You're early." I led the way back into Josie's kitchen. "I didn't expect you until..." I glanced up at the stove and saw that it was already after ten.

"You didn't expect me until now?" Josie laughed. "I'm actually very impressed that the flight was on time and I got out of there so fast. It was seamless. When is travel ever seamless?"

"Never." I laughed. It was good to see Josie, and it was very good to have her there to keep me out of my head so I couldn't keep thinking about—

"Cole!" Josie turned in a circle and hollered her brother's name again before she looked at me. "Where's my big bro? Don't tell me you chased him off."

She knew Josie was only kidding, but her words hit way too close to home. I forced a very fake laugh and busied myself getting my friend a cup of coffee.

"Seriously," Josie asked. "Where is he? I'm dying to see him."

I took a deep breath and handed her the mug of coffee. "You know what...I don't actually know where Cole is. He didn't come home last night, so I assume he met someone in town and—"

"Of course. That sounds just like him. He's never lonely long. Didn't I tell you to keep him away from the women? I should have known he'd—"

"I don't need to hear about it." I knew I was being ridiculous. Especially to Josie, who would have no way to know that my best friend had hooked up with her big brother. And I definitely wasn't about to say anything. But at the same time, I really didn't want to listen to how he was a total player who wouldn't have a cold bed for very long. That I definitely didn't need to hear. "We should probably get some work done around here, right? I mean, you do have a pretty short deadline, right? You might as well use me while you can." I forced a cheer into my voice, I certainly didn't feel. "What should we do first?"

Josie eyed me suspiciously, and for a moment, I was pretty sure she was going to call me on my weirdness. But finally, Josie nodded, followed by a smile. "I have just the thing." She walked down the hall and admired the floor, or lack thereof, and the piles of baseboards and trim Cole and I had made in the living room. "You guys did a bunch," she said. "Thank you. But I have a feeling that today's project is going to be perfect for you right now. Wait here."

She left to go outside, likely to the shed, and I let out the breath I'd been holding in. I hated lying to my best friend, but I wasn't really lying if I just didn't say anything at all, right? Besides, as of tomorrow, it wouldn't matter anymore.

I'd leave, go to Toronto, and leave all of this—and Cole—behind.

Something in my chest ached at the thought of leaving. Not just Josie, but Cole, too. And if I was honest, that was the part that hurt the most. But there really wasn't another option. Unexpected and completely unwanted tears pricked at the back of my eyes. I sniffed hard and forced myself to pull it together just in time for Josie to walk back inside.

She handed me a sledgehammer. "Here."

"What's this for?" I took the hammer and eyed my friend warily.

"Look, I know you, Amber. And I don't know why yet, but I can see that you clearly need a little therapy session. We don't need to talk about it right now," she added quickly, silencing my protest before I could speak it. "There'll be time for that later, but I assume it has something to do with a man, and I gotta tell you, Randy isn't worth any angst at all. I never did like him. And he was never even close to good enough for you." She caught herself and smiled. "But seriously, we'll talk about that douche later. For now, it's time for the next project." She walked through the house to the living room.

I followed, ready to cry again—this time because I had

such a good friend who knew me so well. "What are we going to be doing?"

"This." Josie stopped in front of the wall that separated the tiny living room from the kitchen. "This wall needs to come down. Are you up for it?"

I eyed my friend, and when I saw that she was serious, a small smile crept over my face. I hefted the hammer over my shoulder, ready to swing. "Absolutely."

COLE

I HAD WOKEN BEFORE DAWN, freezing in the cold cab of my truck, and spent the next few hours driving around to warm up before the festival began, and I walked aimlessly around the booths in the square. I'd had at least three cups of apple cider and was only narrowly able to talk my way out of decorating a cupcake. The little girl running the booth was very persistent, and it was hard to say no to six-year-olds in pigtails. But I was in no mood to decorate anything. What I was really in the mood for was some more of that Moon Juice, but I purposely avoided that booth because no good would come from me drinking that delicious beverage before noon on a Sunday. Besides, every time I saw the jars, I thought of Amber and our sleigh ride. It was stupid to have such memories with her after one night, but I couldn't help it. Hell, I couldn't stop thinking about her at all.

After she'd stormed out of the ice castle the night before, I knew I should go after her. But what would I say? It's not as if I could tell her that the last few days I'd spent with her had been some of the best days I'd had in years, maybe ever. I couldn't tell her that the connection I had with her was unlike any I'd ever had with anyone else. And I definitely couldn't tell her that I thought I might be falling in love with her.

No. No way.

I couldn't say any of those things. So, I'd done exactly what I shouldn't have done. I'd let her go. I'd cringed when the door slammed behind me, and then a moment later, I'd looked through the window and watched her run down the street. Later, after enough time had passed, I'd driven past Josie's house and seen the lights on in the upstairs bedroom. Satisfied that she was home safe, I spent the rest of the night driving around the small town until I finally parked my truck in the lot of a local diner and stretched across the front seat to get a few hours of sleep. Not that I managed to get any at all. Whenever I did manage to drift off, I was tortured by images of Amber's face in my dreams.

Cold and tired of attempting to avoid thoughts of Amber, I retreated to the diner and a hot cup of strong coffee. I chose a table in the back where I could stare out the window.

Outside, the sky was gray, and it looked like it might finally snow soon.

Amber would love that. Snow on the last night of the frost festival. It would be perfect.

The thought made me sadder. I stared down into my now cold cup of coffee—how long had I been sitting there? —and tried to think of a way to get Amber out of my head.

I knew it was only a matter of time before I'd have to go to the house. Josie was coming home, and I was going to have to face Amber sooner or later. I'd apologize for basically calling her boring and predictable and generally being a jackass. I couldn't even lie and say that I didn't know why I'd said those things. I did. Everything I'd said was because I meant it. Except for the part where I'd said that Amber was boring. She was far from it. But the life she was choosing was. And I had no idea why she was making the choice she was. She obviously wasn't excited about it. Why was it so hard to choose something different? She didn't even see how much more there was to life. To her. It made me crazy that she couldn't see her own value. To see that she could have a life full of laughter, fun, and living. Because she deserved it. She deserved to wake up every day and laugh, look forward to the adventure, and...

She deserved me.

I dropped my head into my hands and stared at the table-top. I needed more time to figure out what I could say or do to somehow fix things. Not that I thought I'd actually be able to. Not really. The damage was done. I should probably just take off before I cause any more trouble.

"Cole?" I popped my head up in time for Josie's screech to pierce the air. "Cole!"

I jumped up from my chair and met her in the middle of the diner. I wrapped my arms around my baby sister and swung her around as best I could without knocking over the other patrons, who were starting to fill tables for the lunch rush.

"Josie. What are you doing here? When did you get back?"

She pulled back and whacked me on the chest. "I got home hours ago. Nice of you to be there to greet me. And you didn't even answer your phone. I've been calling you all morning."

"Sorry." I shook my head and gestured to my little table. "I've been here. I should have called, Josie. I'm so sorry."

"No," she corrected me. "You should have been at the house. Are you scared of Amber or something? I know she can be a bit fierce when she's in a mood, but she's doing a lot better now that I've had her bashing down walls all morning. I may not know much, but I certainly do know how to work out man problems."

"Man problems?" No way did Amber tell my sister about us. But why wouldn't she? After all, Josie was her best friend, and Amber was really pissed. "What kind of man problems?" I flinched a little bit, waiting for the answer, but breathed a sigh of relief when Josie answered.

"We haven't even talked about it yet, but I assume it's that stupid ex of hers. I mean, he was a total douche, and I really don't think she's dated anyone since him. If you ask me, he didn't even deserve the time he did spend with her. Amber's a pretty special woman and—"

"She is."

Josie stopped and stared at me. She wasn't stupid, and she knew her brother very well, despite the distance we'd had between us over the last few years. "That's right," she said slowly, watching me carefully. "I forget that you've met Amber before, and of course, you just spent the last few days with her." I nodded. "So, where were you last night, brother? No doubt you met some local—"

I didn't have the energy to pretend, and there didn't seem to be any point to it anyway. "We had a fight."

"You had a fight? With Amber?"

I looked around and, for the first time, wondered what my sister was doing in the cafe in the first place. Was Amber with her? "Where is Amber, anyway? What are you doing here?"

"I came to grab some lunch for us. Amber's at home." Josie stepped in front of me, so I had to focus. "I left her bashing a wall down with a sledgehammer to work out some of her feelings that she's clearly having about a man, and please tell me that man is not you, Cole."

I didn't say a word. I didn't have to. I should have known Josie would figure it out in less than five minutes.

"Cole." She smacked my chest with both hands. "No. Please tell me that you're not the reason Amber is back at my house having a whole lot of feelings."

A whole lot of feelings? Because of me? I returned to my

table and sat heavily in the chair before I dropped my head into my hands.

"No, Cole." Josie sat across from me. "Just, no."

They sat in silence for a moment before my sister spoke. "You better tell me what's going on." Her voice was firm, with no room for negotiation. "Now."

I looked up and nodded. "I think I'm falling in love with her." Josie's mouth opened in surprise, but she didn't say anything, so I continued. "I know it sounds crazy, but it's not really if you think about it. The last few days have been…well, it doesn't matter anyway, because she hates me now."

"No. She doesn't hate you. If the way she's swinging that hammer is any indication, she definitely has some strong feelings for you."

"Do you think?" For the first time since Amber had slapped me, I felt something besides defeat. "But then why…I don't understand why she won't even give us a chance?" If anyone understood Amber, it would be Josie. "She's insisting on taking this job, and I know she doesn't want it. I just know it. I offered her—"

"Cole." Josie stopped me with a touch on my arm. "Do you even know why structure is so important to Amber? Why she is the least spontaneous person I know?"

"Of course. I mean, I know that her family…I—" I stopped myself. "No," I admitted. "I guess I don't. Not really."

"You should ask."

My sister's words took me off guard. Of course. I should ask. There were still so many things I didn't know about her. And I wanted to know all of the things.

"I will," I told Josie. "Just as soon as I see her. Well, maybe not right away." I shook my head sharply. "I've really screwed this up, Josie. What should I do?"

"Oh, no." Josie shook her head. "I'm not doing this, Cole. I'm not getting in the middle of anything that the two of you have going. I love you both, and while the idea of the two of you is still really weird...I can't get in the middle." She took a breath and then added, "Except to say one thing."

I couldn't help but laugh. "And what's that, little sis?"

She smiled, but then it faded as she got serious and grabbed my hand across the table. "Whatever's going on with you two, if it means anything...even if you only think it might mean something, don't screw it up, okay?"

"I won't."

"I mean it, Cole. Amber is a good woman. She's not one of your little—"

"I know, Josie. She's so much more."

"She is. And so are you. Don't forget that."

I nodded, the support of my little sister fueling me. "I'm not going to screw it up, but I might need your help."

Chapter Twelve

AMBER

I ASSESSED myself in the mirror and, for at least the dozenth time, questioned what I was doing. All I really wanted to do was curl up on the couch with a bottle of wine and feel sorry for myself. "Why am I doing this again?"

"Because it's the First Frost Festival," Josie called from the bathroom down the hall. "And it's tradition. And you're going to leave tomorrow, and I won't see you for ages." She appeared at the door of the bedroom, and I smiled. "And don't forget, it's mostly because you love me."

"Of course I do." I blew her a kiss and turned back to the mirror so I could tug at my way-too-short dress again. "But I don't think this is the only way to prove that I'm your best friend and love you dearly." I shook my head. "And I'm still not sold on this costume." I grabbed my long red cloak and swung it around my shoulders. "I'm not sure Little Red Riding Hood was supposed to be so…"

"Smokin' hot?" Josie laughed. "Maybe not. But you look great. I, on the other hand, look like an old hag."

Josie did not look like an old hag, but she did look like a grandma. Little Red Riding Hood's grandma, to be exact. I couldn't help but giggle a little at Cole's sense of humor in choosing the costumes.

Earlier, when Josie came home with lunch, she'd also arrived with the costumes Cole had ordered, having run into him in town. But she hadn't come home with Cole. He obviously didn't want to see me. Whatever had happened between us over the last few days obviously hadn't meant the same to him as it had to me. But I couldn't let it bother me. Not tonight.

I'd promised Josie I would go to the Snow Ball with her and have a great night. I couldn't let my feelings about what was obviously not anything to begin with affect that. One more night and I could get on with things, start my new job, and settle into my new life. Besides, if Cole couldn't be bothered to deliver the costumes himself, he wasn't likely to show up at the ball anyway. One less thing I needed to worry about.

I adjusted my dress one last time and fluffed my hair, which cascaded in curls around my shoulders. "I do look good, don't I?"

Josie laughed. "Good? You look hot. Like, really hot. Are you ready to do this?"

"Why not?" I linked arms with my best friend and forced a smile. "Let's go have a great night."

When we got to the party, it was already in full swing. A tent had been put up in the park next to the main town square, which was already packed with people in costume. Twinkle lights and giant snowflakes decorated the space, and it really did look like a winter wonderland. The night was chilly, but with so many people and the heaters throughout the tent, no one seemed to notice. Children ran around, squealing on their hopped-up sugar rushes as they darted from booth to booth, collecting candy just as if it were Halloween. The DJ was pumping tunes over the speakers, and the dance floor was already full. The air was full of festive fun, just as the rest of the weekend had been. I felt a stab of disappointment that Cole wasn't with me to experience the climax of the First Frost Festival. It felt wrong somehow to be there without him.

"Did you talk to your brother?" I hoped the question came off casually.

"I did. When I got the costumes, remember?"

"Oh, right." I was hoping she'd talked to him again. "And what was he doing today? I'm surprised he didn't come by the house."

"You are?" Josie eyed me.

"You're not?" I was having a hard time trying not to look too interested. "I mean, he is here to see you, isn't he? I hope he knows he can be at the house with me there. I mean, I don't want to ruin your visit with him."

"You're not ruining a thing." Josie squeezed my arm. "You know that, right?" I couldn't help but feel that there was more to her question than she was letting on, but I didn't know how much Josie knew or how much she wanted to know about things between Cole and me.

"I know that." I smiled. "But please know I would never want my presence to interfere with your time with your brother, okay? I mean, if he feels awkward in any way because I'm here...well, I just want you to know that whatever reason...look, Josie." I shook my head. I couldn't keep quiet anymore. "I think there's something you should know." I hadn't meant to say anything, but the more I stood there with my best friend, the more I knew that I needed to say something. Josie knew everything about my love life, or more accurately, lack thereof. If it had been anyone else, I would have already told her. But it wasn't anyone else—it was Cole.

Cole.

Just thinking about him left a weird sort of gaping hole in my heart.

"I know, Amber." Josie's voice was kind. "About you and Cole. I mean, I don't know everything, but I do know that I've never seen my big brother as messed up as I saw him earlier. I mean, I've seen him screwed up by a woman before, but never like that. Not even close."

I didn't know whether hearing that should make me feel better or worse.

"And remember, I saw the way you swung that hammer." Josie laughed. "I know pent-up feelings when I see them. I just never would have guessed that they were because of my big brother." She shook her head and laughed. "That is completely new territory for me."

"I know." I grabbed Josie's hand and pulled her aside to a small table where we wouldn't be in the way of all the festivities. "And Josie, you need to understand when I tell you that I never intended for anything to happen. I mean, Cole and I… it's…"

"Crazy?"

I nodded.

"Insane?"

I nodded again.

"Perfect?"

A rush of air escaped my lungs as I almost collapsed into my friend. "Yes."

Josie squealed and wrapped her arms around me in a hug. "I know, right? I mean, at first I wasn't sure. But I think it was just the idea of everything that took me off guard. But the more I think about it, oh my God, yes. It makes perfect sense."

I laughed a little. "It actually makes no sense at all. We're total opposites in every way."

Josie didn't disagree, but she didn't agree either. Instead, she took my hands and squeezed.

"It doesn't matter anyway." I shook my head. "We argued, and he said things, and I said things, and now...well...it doesn't matter anymore. I'm leaving tomorrow to start my new job. I told you about that, right? I was offered the job at Wallace and McKwade, and even though I didn't formally accept it, I kind of did and—"

"Congratulations."

"It is a good job, Josie."

"I said congratulations."

"It really is a great job," I spoke to my friend, but I could no longer be sure of who exactly I was trying to convince. "It's really everything I've ever wanted, and most people would kill for such an offer."

"I'm sure they would."

"I should be thrilled. Celebrating. This is a job that anyone would be super lucky to get right out of school. It's a huge deal, Josie."

"I believe you."

"I should be so happy."

"But you're not."

I looked around the busy square filled with people, hoping against hope to see Cole standing there waiting for me. "No," I said softly. "I'm not."

"You know what I think?"

I looked at my friend, hoping for some grand revelation.

"I think we need to dance."

I laughed. "I actually can't think of a better idea right now."

I let Josie lead me through the crowd to the dance floor, where she pulled me into her arms. I laughed again. "We must look crazy," I said. "Granny and Little Red Riding Hood dancing together."

Josie spun me around before she pulled me back in for a dip. "We don't look any crazier than anyone else here," Josie said. "It's a Halloween-themed Snow Ball, for God's sake."

"True." I found myself laughing harder than I had in a long time as Josie continued to take the lead, swinging me and moving me around the dance floor. She spun me hard, extending my arm so it sent me spinning along the floor until a strong pair of arms caught me. Instantly, my body both simultaneously tensed and melted from relief. I looked up into the eyes of the Big Bad Wolf.

"My, what beautiful eyes you have."

COLE

I HELD HER TIGHT, afraid Amber would slap me again. Or worse, bolt. Once I had her back in my arms, I had no intention of letting go. I could feel her body tense when I caught her. But she wasn't pulling away.

Finally, she looked up into my eyes. "Isn't that my line?"

I didn't answer right away, choosing instead to move her slowly around the dance floor to the romantic lyrics of the latest Thomas Rhett song. "You do have beautiful eyes."

"The better to see you with, my dear."

I laughed. "That's my line."

She shrugged. "It's an interesting costume choice."

I wore a full wolf suit with a half mask over my face. I hadn't been so sure about it at first, but the effect was actually pretty impressive, even with the granny hat and gown over my wolf suit.

I spun her easily and pulled her back into my chest, where I preferred her. "I thought they were fitting. Given the situation."

"And what situation is that?" She looked up at me through thick, dark lashes that made her look every bit the part of the innocently sexy Little Red Riding Hood.

I had to force myself to stay calm and move slowly when all I really wanted to do was twirl her right off the dance floor and into a private corner where I could tell her all the things I'd been thinking since the last moment I'd seen her. I wanted to take her and hold her until she understood that whatever was going on between us was real, even if neither of us understood it yet. They couldn't ignore it, and not even some stupid thing I'd said when I'd been upset and not thinking straight should keep them from figuring it all out. I wanted to kiss her until she felt exactly what I was trying to say.

But it wasn't the time to do any of that. We were in costume, and I'd play the role. I'd play it as long as it took to convince her that whatever it was that I was feeling for her, it was real.

I grinned widely, knowing my costume likely made me look as wolfish and sinister as possible. "The situation between the innocent good girl and the wicked bad boy."

I could tell she was trying not to, but a smile crept across her face. "I'm the innocent good girl?"

"Innocent enough." I spun her around again. The twinkling lights strung around the dance floor sparkled and danced on her skin. "And I'm definitely bad enough."

"Enough for what?"

I paused mid-turn and held her fast. "Enough to make this work."

"This?"

"Us. The innocent girl and the Big Bad Wolf."

She shook her head. "That's not how the story goes."

The music changed pace to a more upbeat song, and I

easily transitioned into a quicker step, moving Amber around the dance floor through the crowd, but I didn't release my grip on her. "If I remember correctly, the Big Bad Wolf pursued Little Red Riding Hood until she finally gave in."

"That's an interesting take on it," Amber said. "If you call stalking and hunting pursuing."

I gave her another grin. "Maybe I do. If it gets me the girl in the end."

Amber's smile faded, and she shook her head slightly. "That's not how the story goes. He didn't get the girl at all. The woodsman came and saved Little Red Riding Hood from the Big Bad Wolf. He took the wolf out to the forest, and she never heard from him again."

Dammit. I hadn't thought that part of the fairy tale through. But it was just that. A fairy tale. Having Amber standing in front of me—that was real. The way she made me feel—that was real. Everything about us and the last few days —that was very real. She wasn't going to get off on a technicality. This was too important.

With two fingers, I tilted her chin up so she was looking at me. No, she was looking at my wolf mask. It wasn't good enough. I kept one hand on her back, and with the other, I pulled off my mask so she was looking at my face. I couldn't be sure, but I had to believe that she'd be able to see the truth in my eyes. "That doesn't matter," I said after a moment. "None of that matters."

"Of course it matters."

"No." We'd stopped moving, and couples danced around us, but I didn't care. The only thing I cared about was the woman in front of me and fixing things between us. There was no way I was going to let her walk away from whatever it was we'd started. "It doesn't matter, Amber, because we're going to write our own ending."

She tried to look down, but I wouldn't let her. I cupped her cheek and held her so our eyes were locked.

"It will never work, Cole. I'm—"

"It will." I nodded. "You're a planner. You're a rule follower, and you're responsible. I'm the exact opposite of that. I've never planned anything in my life, and I definitely don't follow the rules." I winked at her, and that got a smile, but I could see the unshed tear in her eye.

"That's why this can never work." The tear rolled down her cheek. "We're so different, Cole. We come from different places. I just don't see how…"

I couldn't stand it anymore. I lowered my mouth to her lips and kissed her gently. "We'll write our own ending," I repeated. "This is our story. We get to decide how it ends, Amber. Or at the very least, we get to write the next chapter. And whatever it looks like, I want my story to include you."

"But…Australia…you…I'm…"

"Tell me you don't want me."

She shook her head, and another tear slipped down her cheek. "I can't." A smile tugged at the corner of her mouth. "I can't tell you that, because I do want you. So much."

I didn't need to hear anything else. I slipped a hand behind her head and pulled her to my mouth, where I kissed her like I'd never kissed before. In fact, I could have quite happily spent the rest of the night kissing her if that's what it took, but someone had other plans.

"I'm going to go out on a limb here and guess that you two have sorted yourselves out." Josie's voice distracted me.

"Damn, little sis. You make a frighteningly good granny," I said when I finally pulled myself away from Amber.

She smacked me on the arm. "I can rock whatever costume you give me." She glanced between us. "But seriously." Her face shifted back to one lined with concern. "Are you two good? Can we dance? I mean, you are both here to see me, aren't you?"

"Well, I don't know—"

"Of course—"

We laughed as the DJ started playing a popular dance tune. I took them each by the hand and spun them around. As much as I wanted to get Amber alone, my sister wanted to party, and I owed her. There'd be plenty of time for me to get Amber alone later. Right now, I'd settle for having her hand in mine, back where it belonged.

Chapter Thirteen

AMBER

IT WAS late by the time we got back to Josie's house. My feet ached from hours of dancing, but I didn't care. We'd had a great night, introducing Josie to Moon Juice and even decorating cupcakes that we then ate in a few bites. It had been a perfect night. When we got back to the house, Josie had offered to share her bed with me, but she'd done so with a laugh, because we all knew Cole would never let that happen.

After Josie retreated upstairs, together we'd created a makeshift bed on the floor from the couch cushions and a pile of quilts. It wasn't the most comfortable bed I'd slept on, but I didn't care because Cole's arms were wrapped around me, and I'd never been happier.

Except maybe when he suddenly flipped me so I lay on my back and looked up into his eyes.

"You were the most beautiful Little Red Riding Hood I've

ever seen." He kissed my nose. "And you were definitely the sexiest woman there tonight."

"Is that right?"

"Oh, that's right." He kissed me again, only this time his kiss was more demanding, needing more. I moaned and closed my eyes, more than ready to take the kiss further. But as quickly as it started, it ended.

I snapped my eyes open and stared at him.

"I meant what I said earlier, Amber," Cole said. "About writing our own story. We get to choose what happens next. Do you believe that?"

I nodded.

"I don't know how…or…" He stopped himself with a shake of his head. "All I know is that I want to be with you."

I reached up and wrapped my arms around his neck. "And I want to be with you." I tugged him closer so I could kiss him. "Now."

He didn't need any more invitation than that, and this time when our lips came together, I kissed him with a need that had been building up since the night before. I slipped my hands up and over his hard, muscled back. I squeezed and pulled, needing him as close to me as I could get him.

"You're very demanding." He grinned a little as he pulled back.

"You have no idea." I laughed.

"I like it." He dropped his head to my neck, where he nipped and licked the skin there. "A lot."

Cole kept up the kisses and licks as he worked his way down to my breasts. His hot mouth on my bare skin fueled me. Everything about being with Cole was exciting. He woke feelings in me that I never knew I had. How had I gone my entire life and never felt the way I felt with him?

The litany of questions about our future together that I'd been suppressing all night tried to sneak its way to the forefront of my mind. Where were we going to live? What about my job? Would Cole move to Toronto for me? Did I want him to? What about Australia? What would my family say?

Before I could let myself go too far down that rabbit hole, a sharp sensation that straddled the line between pleasure and pain brought me back to the moment. I blinked hard and focused on Cole, poised above me, one hand cupping my right breast, my nipple between two of his fingers.

"Stay with me," he said simply. "Stay out of your head, Amber."

He waited until I nodded and then sucked my nipple into his mouth, causing every other thought to be pushed straight out of my head. There wasn't room for anything but the sensations tearing through my body.

I squirmed, and my climax grew quickly and unexpectedly.

"Cole," I whispered on a moan. "I need..." I didn't bother to finish the sentence, letting my hand that had slid between us and found his hard cock do the talking instead. I squeezed and stroked, and a moment later, it was Cole who was doing the moaning.

"Dammit, woman."

I grinned as he lifted his head to meet my gaze again. There was fire in his eyes, and just seeing how much he wanted me fired me up even more.

I wiggled my hips and pressed myself up to him.

Cole groaned again and reached over my head to the coffee table. He grabbed the condom and made quick work of sheathing himself before positioning himself at my hot core, but only for a moment before he pushed inside me.

I cried out. The feel of him inside me was...everything. It was only belatedly that I remembered that Josie was sleeping only one floor away. I bit my lip as he moved inside me, bringing me right to the edge of an orgasm that would not be held back.

I wrapped my legs around his back in an effort to keep him even closer.

"Let go, babe." He kissed me, but only for a moment before the waves of ecstasy started to crash through me. To keep from crying out, I tucked my head into his neck and dug my fingers into his back.

A moment later, he joined me in his own release. Slowly, we pulled away from each other and shifted so that Cole lay behind me. I tucked up tightly against his chest. Cole kept his arm wrapped tightly around me and dropped little kisses along my shoulder and the back of my neck as I drifted off to sleep.

I'D MANAGED to go the entire night without giving any thought to what would happen in the morning, but now, still snuggled against his hard, naked chest, as the warm glow of the morning sun started to fill the room, I could no longer ignore the questions that popped up in my head.

"What are you thinking?" Cole kissed the back of my head.

I hadn't even known he was awake.

"How do you know I'm thinking about something?"

He chuckled. "Babe, it doesn't take a genius to see that you're busy overthinking something."

I twisted in his arms. "I'm not overthinking. I'm just thinking. I mean…" I trailed off, unsure how to say what I needed to without ruining the perfect night we'd had.

"Just say it. There's no point keeping it inside now," he said. "And besides that, I'm pretty sure I already know what you're thinking."

Maybe he did, maybe he didn't. But either way, it wasn't going to be easy to talk about. Especially considering I had zero experience talking about what it was I wanted to do. I was in completely uncharted territory.

After a moment, I nodded. "We do. I mean, what happens next, Cole? Are you coming with me to Toronto? I'm supposed to start my job next week."

He was quiet for a moment, but finally, he said, "If that's what you want, I will absolutely come with you."

"You will?"

"Sure. I've never been to Toronto." He didn't hesitate with his answer, and my heart swelled unexpectedly. Randy never would have moved for me. It was too soon to think of whatever it was with Cole as a relationship, but...whatever it was, it was nice. I turned and propped myself up on my arm to look at him.

"This is crazy."

"What? Moving to Toronto? I agree." He shrugged. "But I've done crazier things."

"No. Well, yes. That too." I laughed even though I felt like crying. "But that's not what I mean."

"What do you mean?"

"You. This." I shook my head. "Us. We're talking about tomorrow." I gestured wildly between us. "We're talking about...well, more." It sounded so stupid and so completely insane to say it out loud, but I didn't care.

"We are." Cole took my hand and pulled me down to him.

"And that doesn't scare you?"

He laughed. "It scares the hell out of me." It took a moment, but then he shook his head and added, "Look. I've never lived my life with any kind of plan. It drove my parents crazy." He rolled his eyes. "I've always just gone with the flow of things, and if it felt right, I did it."

The very idea of going with the flow, the way Cole just described, scared the hell out of me. But deep down, it also excited a part of me. A big part.

"And I don't know about Toronto," Cole continued. "But I do know that this feels right." He took my hand and pressed it to his chest. "If you really want to take that job, then okay. I'll go. I want to be with you, and if that means Toronto, then that's what it means."

"What about Australia?"

"It's not going anywhere. We'll go another time."

"But it was only the other night that you asked me to go with you. Now you're willing to come with me?"

He nodded. "Of course, as I said, I've done crazier things than following a woman who I..."

My heart did a strange flutter in my chest. "Who you're... *what*?"

What was he going to say?

He shook his head and smiled. "Who I think is super sexy."

The words were meant to be teasing and fun, but they fell flat, and I couldn't help but think that there'd been something else he'd been about to say. But I wouldn't push. Because what if he didn't feel the same way I did? Sure, I knew he liked me. Enough to throw up his whole life in the air, and that was definitely something. But was it everything?

Was it enough?

Was it love?

And did it even matter?

Chapter Fourteen

COLE

"I THINK IT'S AWESOME." Josie sat across the table from us, sipping her coffee as if it were no big deal that they'd just told her I was moving to Toronto. My sister never failed to surprise me. "Are you surprised?" Josie looked between us. "I mean, just because I sort of said I wasn't sure about it, you didn't really think I'd disapprove of all this?" She waved her hand between us and laughed. "You did, didn't you?"

Amber shrugged, but I answered. "Honestly? Kind of. I mean, I'm your big brother."

"And I'm your best friend."

"And that's exactly why it's perfect." Josie laughed and drank her coffee. "Who else would I want for my sister-in-law?"

"Whoa!"

"What?"

We both spoke at the same time, and when Amber looked

at me with panic on her face, I patted her hand and smiled. "No one is saying anything about marriage."

"Yet."

"Josie. Seriously. We're talking about Toronto. That's it." I needed to shut my sister down before she got any more crazy ideas. And marriage was crazy. I'd barely gotten used to the idea that I was falling for this girl. Never mind spending the rest of my life with her. Way too soon for that.

"And we're not making any plans."

I turned and looked at Amber with shock and admiration. For a girl who'd planned her whole life, she was coming over quickly to my way of thinking. I liked it. More importantly, I liked her. A lot.

So much so that it scared me.

"Whatever you say. Either way, I'm happy for you guys," Josie said. "But there's only one thing."

"What's that?"

"This house." She moaned and then laughed. "I was counting on your help."

I instantly felt a flash of guilt. "I know. I'm so sorry. Do you want me to stay?" I looked quickly between my sister and Amber, who nodded. "I'll stay. What do you need me to do?"

"No." She waved her arm in the air. "Amber has a job to get to." I didn't think I was imagining it when I saw Amber flinch, but before I could say anything, Josie continued talking. "I'll be fine. I'm just being sensitive. But I will miss you both." Josie jumped up from the table. "Now come and give me a hug before I change my mind and make you stay."

AMBER

LEAVING Josie was harder than I expected. There hadn't been enough time to spend with my friend. I'd almost turned my car around twice to go back and spend a few more days with her, but ultimately, I'd kept going, following Cole in his truck. With two rental vehicles, we had to drive separately back to Saskatoon and the airport. I would rather have been with Cole. I couldn't get enough of him.

You'll have plenty of time to be with him in Toronto.

Toronto.

At my new job. It was what I'd wanted. A good job at a prestigious firm. It would be a great start to my career. It was perfect. Even more so, Cole decided to go with me. Sure, I hadn't planned that part of things, but it didn't matter. I could go with the flow. That in itself surprised me so much I had to laugh. Me, go with the flow? It was crazy how only a few days could change so much.

But even with all the changes—or maybe because of them —something still wasn't sitting right with me. I should be thrilled that I was getting everything I wanted, but whenever I tried to picture myself walking into Wallace and McKwade, I couldn't.

Maybe it was because I hadn't formally accepted the job. But more likely it was because I was no longer sure it was what I wanted. After all, did I really want to turn into a workaholic who spent all my waking hours crunching numbers and poring over financial statements?

And then there was Cole. We hadn't discussed what he was going to do in Toronto. In fact, I had no idea what he was trained to do. Had he even graduated from college? I didn't think so. I remembered Josie saying something about how he'd dropped out halfway through to travel to Australia. Not that it mattered, not really. Besides, Cole didn't seem concerned about what he'd do.

But I was.

Because the longer I drove, the harder it was to imagine Cole in a big city, working some kind of corporate job where he'd be miserable. He would hate it there. He needed an adventure, or at least somewhere with open spaces, no buildings to fence him in. He'd resent me. And then…

By the time we pulled up to the rental car return and dropped off our keys, I was fixated on the idea that no matter what he said, Cole didn't belong in the big city with me.

"What's going on in that pretty head?" he asked me as we walked through the airport hand in hand in search of the desk where Cole could change his ticket. "You seem a million miles away, and that's worrying me a little bit."

I shrugged. "I'm fine. I'm just thinking." He grabbed my hand and pulled me to a stop before I realized what was happening.

"What's going on?" he demanded.

I shook my head and was about to protest and say something that would smooth things over, but I changed my mind and said what I knew was right. "We can't go to Toronto."

"What?"

Once the words were out of my mouth, I finally felt as though I could breathe again.

"What are you talking about? Your job is there."

"No."

"It is."

"Yes, I mean, no." I stopped and smiled before continuing. "What I mean is, I don't want to go there. I didn't even really formally accept the job, and I'm not even excited about it. In fact, I'm kind of dreading it."

Cole's face twisted up in confusion for a moment before he said, "So what are you thinking?"

"I don't want to go to Toronto."

He laughed but didn't release my hands. "Okay. So what do you want?"

"You," I answered without hesitation. "I want you."

"But not the job?"

I shook my head. "No."

"Australia?"

I shrugged. "I don't know." It was an honest answer.

"Okay." Cole drew the word out. "So, you know you want me?" I nodded. "You don't want the job?" I shook my head. "And you're not sure about Australia?"

"Right."

"So, what do we do?" He looked around. "We can't stay here. I mean, we could go back to Crystal Creek and—"

"Cedar Springs." The idea popped into my head, but the moment it did, it felt right. My family had been wanting me to go visit, and the holidays were coming. Besides, it's not as if we had any other place to go. "My whole family is there right now," I explained. "It's complicated, but I have a few brothers I don't really know, and they're all there, and they all seem to be married or getting married and...why not?" I finished with a shrug.

Cole eyed me carefully. "Did you plan this?"

I smacked him playfully on the shoulder. "Not at all."

"Then I think it's perfect. Let's go to Cedar Springs."

"Really?"

"Do you really think I'd say no?" He grinned, and I stood on my tiptoes to kiss him. "Hell, I was ready to go to Toronto for you. I think I can go to Cedar Springs." He shook his head with a chuckle. "Besides, I'd like to meet your family."

Meet my family.

The words echoed in my head as I thought of not only Chelsea, Cal, and Declan, but also of the two half-brothers I didn't know. The ones who'd never wanted me in their lives. Until now.

"Me too," I said with a shaky smile. "Me too."

Chapter Fifteen

COLE

REMEMBERING the look on Josie's face when I'd told her that we were leaving, I suggested a compromise. We'd go back to Crystal Creek for a few weeks and help Josie with as much work on the house as we could, before going to Cedar Springs in time for Christmas.

It was the perfect plan.

A word I was starting to get used to, even if I still did like teasing Amber about it.

The best part of the few weeks we spent in Crystal Creek with my little sister wasn't catching up with Josie—although that part was fantastic and made me miss her even more. It wasn't getting my hands dirty demolishing walls, ripping up more flooring, and putting fresh coats of paint on all the walls —although it was satisfying to see the transformation of the old house. It wasn't even sleeping with Amber wrapped tight in my arms every night—but that was a very close second.

No, the best part of our time in Crystal Creek was watching Amber come alive. Despite the fact that her life had taken a very sharp and very unexpected turn, she seemed to blossom with the lack of structure to their days. She didn't have to get up and go to an office, didn't have to sit and crunch numbers all day—although she swore she loved that part—and for the first time in her life, didn't have to follow some sort of grand master plan for her life.

For me, just watching the way she laughed more, smiled more easily, and danced through each day made me fall for her a little bit more. Not that I could fall much more. I was already completely lost to her. In fact, I was pretty sure that my heart had been completely hers from the moment she pressed her back up against the wall and wielded a remote control at me.

It was a revelation that was equal parts terrifying and exciting. Yes. I was definitely falling in love with her. But I wasn't ready to share my feelings for her. Not yet.

I leaned against the door of my rental truck after making one last trip out to the car with Amber's bags.

Why couldn't I tell her?

It was a question that had been driving me crazy for days now, but I didn't have any real answer. Not beyond the cop-out that I was waiting for her to say it first. I'd never been that kind of guy. If there was something I wanted, I went after it. If there was something that needed to be said, I said it.

Of course, I'd never felt the way I felt about Amber before. I'd never remotely felt as if I might be in love or falling in love or whatever it was that I was feeling. It scared the hell out of me.

And that was it. I was scared. Never in my life had I put myself out there the way I had with Amber. What if she rejected me? What if she changed her mind? What if...

It turned into forever?

I'd spent my whole adult life running from the life my

parents wanted for me. The life they had. Nice enough. Hadn't that been how I'd described it to Amber? Was I choosing that now? By giving up my life of freedom to put someone else's needs before my own, was I turning into the very thing I'd been trying to prevent?

The thought slammed into me, and I had to take a step back from the truck. I inhaled the crisp December air and forced myself to breathe slowly.

This was different. I was not turning into everything I'd been running from.

And so what if I was?

As I turned, I caught a glimpse of the object of my confused thoughts inside, giving Josie a hug. We were headed to the airport soon. This time for real. Flights were booked, and it was time to move on. At least as far as Cedar Springs and Amber's family. She hadn't said much about how she was feeling about visiting her family, but I could tell it was weighing on her. And how could it not? From what I understood, her two oldest half-brothers had never wanted anything to do with Amber or her sister until recently. They blamed the girls for their father's betrayal.

I shook my head. The whole situation was screwed up. But from what I understood, the siblings had not only made peace with their parents' decisions, but had actually formed a tight family bond. Not that super close families were really my thing, but I had a feeling that Amber would love it.

Once she got over her nerves about it all, that was.

"Are you ready?" The women appeared outside in the cold morning, their faces red from crying.

"It's not like you're not going to see each other again." I smiled. I hated good-byes. Especially when they involved tears.

"I'm ready." Amber wiped her cheeks and forced a smile. "I don't know what's wrong with me," she said. "I'm usually not so emotional."

"It's because you usually know exactly what's happening next." Josie pulled her back in for one more hug, and I did my best not to roll my eyes.

"She does know what's happening next," I said. "We're going to Cedar Springs for the holiday."

Amber pulled away from Josie and stared at her. "Are you sure you don't want to come? I don't want you to be alone for the holidays."

This time, I didn't try to stop the eye roll. We'd already been over this. At least a dozen times. Josie was going to stay in Crystal Creek for Christmas before joining our parents for the New Year. Because after all, someone had to represent the Price children. And I had no intention of making another stop in my hometown. Although the idea of introducing my parents to Amber as my girlfriend and not just my sister's best friend was appealing. Despite my frustration with them, I couldn't seem to completely shut off the little part of me that still wanted to make them happy in some way. And I knew without a doubt that seeing me with a woman as amazing as Amber would make them very happy indeed.

But it wasn't the right time.

One family at a time.

"I'm fine," Josie was telling Amber for the hundredth time.

"Okay." Amber gave her one last look. "I'll let you two say good-bye." She turned quickly and disappeared into the cab of the truck. Likely before she could start crying again.

As soon as she was gone, Josie turned to me. She gave me such a strange look that after a moment, I shook my head and forced a laugh. "What?"

"I just needed a minute to really look at you so I could be sure."

"Sure of what?"

"That you're in love."

"Whoa!" I held up my hands and took a step back. "No one is saying anything about—"

"Stop it. You're talking to me, remember?" Josie took a step forward and grabbed my hands. "Besides, it's not like I didn't know it already. I mean, it would have to take some pretty strong feelings to get you to give it all up."

"Australia?"

"The bachelor life you were so certain would bring you happiness."

I shrugged in an effort to appear a whole lot more casual than I actually was. "I think I might have been wrong about what would make me happy." I turned and glanced toward the truck, where Amber dabbed at her eyes and looked out the window away from us. "In fact, I'm pretty sure I was."

"I can't tell you how great it feels to see you so smitten, big brother." Josie threw her arms around me and squeezed. "Now, go. I don't want to be the reason you guys miss your flight." She released me and took a quick step back. "And one more thing, Cole." Josie gestured to the truck with her head. "Be careful with her. She's way more nervous about meeting her brothers than she's letting on."

"How do you—"

"I know."

AMBER

IT WAS an uneventful flight to Calgary, but a slightly more eventful drive through the icy mountain roads to Cedar Springs a few hours away deep in the Rockies. Despite the fact that he'd been in sunny Australia for a few years, Cole handled the icy, snow-covered roads like a pro, and soon we were in the valley that would lead us into town.

"What do you remember about Cedar Springs?"

I laughed. "Nothing. I only came here once when I was a kid. I was too young to really remember anything but the beach. It wasn't until years later, when everything came out about my dad and his other family, that I realized how messed up it was that we would have been here at all. Because while my mom knew about them, they didn't know about us. And certainly, Chelsea and I didn't know anything."

"So why were you here?"

I shook my head and shrugged. "I don't really know. Now, looking back, I think Dad wanted to be discovered, even back then. I mean, how insane would it be, having two families?"

Cole shook his head. "I can't wrap my head around it," he said. "I still think that story is absolutely unbelievable."

"You and me both." I looked out the window and took in the snowy mountain peaks and the thick forest that surrounded us. It had been way too long since I'd been in the mountains.

Despite the cold winter air outside, I unrolled the window and let the fresh air blast inside. It did little to soothe my nerves that had become progressively more frayed since we'd landed. Chelsea had done her best to reassure me that Mitch and Ian were great guys and were excited to meet me properly. But no matter what my little sister said, I couldn't shake the feeling that I was about to walk into the viper's den.

Cedar Springs was their territory. They didn't like me. Well, maybe they did. Or they would…or…whatever…

I took a deep breath and then another.

"Hey, are you okay?" Cole slid his hand over my thigh and squeezed. His touch brought me back to the moment.

"I'm fine."

He gave me a look, but then quickly returned his gaze to the icy road in front of him.

"I am," I said again, even though he didn't ask. "I just

needed a bit of fresh air." I forced a cheeriness into my voice, and it seemed to appease him.

"It's certainly fresh out there." He unrolled his own window. "It's downright freezing."

The blast of icy air only lasted a few moments before we were both shivering, and we once again put our windows up.

"It may be cold," Cole said. "But it sure is beautiful here. I'm looking forward to trying some snowboarding."

"You are?"

"You don't snowboard?"

I shook my head. Of course, I didn't snowboard. It was dangerous. Really dangerous. My parents had always tried to get me to join them at Whistler, a ski resort just outside of Vancouver, but I had always opted to stay home while Chelsea took them up on their offer. I was way less likely to break a leg if I didn't strap myself to a board and point it down a mountain.

Had I always been so boring?

Sadly, I knew the answer to that. I had. And maybe it was time that I stopped blaming my past for that. After all, one could only blame their parents' life choices for the outcome of their lives for so long.

I sighed, but quickly covered it up with a smile.

"But I'll try it," I said before I could overthink it.

"You will?"

I couldn't be sure who was more surprised. But once I'd said it out loud, it actually sounded like a good idea. "I totally will."

Cole slipped his hand in mine and squeezed. "You're full of surprises, Amber."

That was the truth. I hardly recognized myself lately. No job, no plan, no... "That's the turn," I told Cole, interrupting my own internal thoughts, which was probably a good thing because they always led to the same place—a mild panic attack.

Okay, a panic attack that was beginning to grow in intensity each time.

At some point, I was going to have to figure out the future. But today wasn't that day. "Right here." I pointed to the turn, and consulted the instructions that Chelsea had given me. We were going to meet at the neighborhood pub, the Grizzly Paw.

Chelsea had moved in with her new boyfriend, and apparently, that left an empty room at our half-brother Mitch's house, as well as a room at our oldest brother Ian's house, which happened to be the house where my half-brothers, growing up, had spent their summers. When I heard that, I knew that there was no way Cole and I could stay there. After all, that was the house they'd been in when they'd found out about my father's deception.

How could I stay there knowing that?

How could I stay with either of them?

Once again, I was filled with indecision. Maybe we were doing the wrong thing? After all, we'd been happy enough going along without meeting. Why should that change now?

But we were here, and Cole was making the turn down the road that would lead us to my family. All of my family.

Besides, it wasn't as if we had to stay with either Mitch or Ian. I had two other brothers. Declan was living with his fiancée, Evie, and her son, Jonah. Which meant there really was only one option left—Cal. He was close to me in age, and we'd been friends in our teenage years, although we'd lost touch a little bit lately as Cal's movie star career had taken him all over the world on jobs. Of course, now he, too, was settled into Cedar Springs, filming a show based on Ian and his fiancée, Gwen's life.

I hadn't said it outright, but I was hoping that Chelsea had read between the lines and would secure us a room with Cal and his fiancée, Milena, for the holiday.

Maybe I should have said it outright? Yes. I should have. I never should have left something like that to chance.

"Maybe we can get a room at that new resort?" I blurted it before I could think it through. "I mean, it's probably really expensive, but—"

Cole squeezed my hand. "Whatever you want to do," he said. "We'll stay wherever you want to."

I nodded and turned to the window again.

My eyes took in the giant pine wreaths attached to the light poles, complete with huge red bows, and my heart raced. A cold sweat pricked at the back of my neck, and my hands clenched into fists in my lap. I forced myself to take deep breaths.

"It will be okay." Cole squeezed my hand again. "I know you're nervous," he said calmly. "But they want to meet you." He sounded so sure of himself, even though there was no way he could know that. Not really. "Chelsea wouldn't have invited you for Christmas if it wasn't going to be okay. You know that."

I did know that. But there'd been so many changes lately. Maybe I shouldn't have thrown my family into the mix, too. Maybe we should just keep driving and—

Cole pulled the rental truck up in front of a large timber-framed building. A wooden sign declaring it the Grizzly Paw hung out front.

"We're here."

Chapter Sixteen

COLE

AS WE STEPPED TOGETHER through the massive wooden doors to the Grizzly Paw pub, Amber tightened her grip on my hand. She was worried. Of course she was worried. Who wouldn't be?

But as worried as she was, I knew logically—just as I was sure she knew—everything would be okay. I'd meant what I'd said in the car. Her sister wouldn't have invited her if their brothers wouldn't be welcoming.

Even so, I wasn't naive enough to think that my words would be enough. Hopefully my support would be.

"You got this," I whispered into her ear before pressing a small kiss to her cheek.

She offered a small smile in return only moments before a shorter, dark-haired version of Amber descended on us.

Chelsea.

It was easy to see the family resemblance between them,

but it only took me seconds to notice the one marked difference as Chelsea squealed out a greeting and pulled her sister out of my grasp and into a tight hug. Chelsea was by far the more outgoing of the sisters. Even if Amber hadn't told me about her little sister's penchant for making bad choices and being the rebel when they were younger, it would have been easy to see. What was also easy to see was their love for each other.

Her uncertainty was obviously forgotten—at least for the moment—as Amber embraced her sister. They spoke a series of rapid and completely incoherent things at each other and broke out into a mixture of laughter and tears.

There was definitely something about sisters.

A few moments later, the women were joined by two men who jumped straight into the fray and wrapped their arms around the crying, laughing women before squeezing them into a tight bear hug.

Completely abandoned, I might have started feeling a little out of place with the mini family reunion, if I wasn't enjoying it so much. It was yet another side of Amber I hadn't seen before. And just like everything else I knew about her, I loved it.

"You must be Cole."

The voice startled me, and I turned to see a petite, curvy woman dressed in a long sweater and leggings smiling up at me. She stuck out her hand and grinned. "I'm Milena." She used her head to nod to the group as I shook her hand. "Cal's fiancée. I'm glad you guys could come for Christmas. I've heard so much about...well, I've heard a lot about Amber," she corrected herself, the smile never leaving her face. "But I have to admit, nobody has said much about you."

"That's because I'm new." I smiled broadly. "Very new. But I'm really happy to be here. And this..." I shook my head with a smile at the siblings still hugging. "This is pretty awesome to see."

Milena put her hand on my arm, and together we took a step back. "I think it's about to get better." She pointed subtly to two other men who'd approached. The family resemblance was very strong between all the McCormick brothers, and there was no doubt at all that the two men who stood together, looking both hopeful and apprehensive, were Ian and Mitch. The two oldest McCormick brothers. The ones Amber was so nervous about seeing.

Instinctively, I took a step forward. To what? Protect her? But that was ridiculous. There was nothing threatening about them. If anything, they looked just as nervous as Amber had been in the car. Possibly more.

I stepped back again as one of the men cleared his voice and said, "Amber?"

The hugging and crying in front of us stopped. Slowly, the other siblings moved away and left Amber to face the two oldest brothers alone. I crossed my arms over my chest, both to keep myself from going to her as well as in a defensive move. I knew I needed to let Amber handle this, but if either of them hurt her, or made her cry, or…well, they'd have me to deal with.

The shot of protectiveness surprised me because Amber definitely wasn't the type of woman who needed protecting in any way, and besides my sister when we were kids, I had never felt any type of protectiveness toward a woman before. It was unexpected. But it felt right.

I once again took a step forward.

This time, Milena put her hand on my arm and squeezed. "It's fine," she said, as if everything I was thinking was written on my face. Maybe it was. "I think Mitch and Ian are just as nervous as she is. But they're also very excited. It's been a big year around here, and while I don't know everything about all of this, I can tell you with certainty— they all have huge hearts, and everyone is ready to put their father's choices behind them and move on. Amber was the missing piece."

I studied Amber's face carefully as she looked upon her oldest brothers. Her initial response of wariness was very quickly replaced with a shaky smile. That was all I saw, because only seconds later, the two men pulled her into a giant hug and she was swallowed up by them.

I hardly had a moment to recover from the raw emotion I'd just witnessed before Chelsea was in front of me.

"You must be Cole." She grabbed me, wrapped her arms around me, and squeezed.

I didn't know much about the McCormicks, but my first impression was that they were a family who liked to hug.

The loving feeling didn't last long, as Chelsea pulled back and smacked me hard in the arm. "I can't believe you convinced her not to take that job!"

I rubbed at my arm, suddenly unsure whether this woman was going to hit me again, because damn, that was a hard—and totally unexpected—smack.

"I didn't convince her not to do anything." I shook my head and looked toward Amber, who was completely absorbed in a conversation with Ian and Mitch and not at all concerned about me or the abuse her sister was doling out. "I swear, I—"

"I think it's great!"

Chelsea laughed and I tipped my head in question. "You do?"

"I do." She grinned. "You didn't think I was mad at you, did you?"

"Honestly?"

"Whatever." Chelsea shook her head. "Come on, I'll introduce you to everyone else."

AMBER

IN ALL THE ways I'd imagined the reunion taking place, I never could have imagined it would go so well. Well, maybe I could have years ago when I'd first heard about my brothers. I'd been so naive then, thinking that they would all be just as excited for the expansion of my family as I was. They'd rejected me all those years ago. Of course, they'd only been kids. Young and confused and so very hurt.

Time changed things. And it definitely had changed things between the McCormick siblings. More than once throughout the night, I had caught myself staring at Ian and Mitch and shaking my head as if I couldn't actually believe we were all together finally. It seemed surreal, as if I were in a dream.

Sitting at the Grizzly Paw, Cole and I were introduced to so many people, my head spun as I worked to keep the names and faces straight. I opted to leave my drink untouched and instead clung to Cole's hand under the table like a lifeline tethering me to the present. Even so, the night was long and completely overwhelming, but also equal parts awesome.

It was Declan, always a little bit more tuned in than the others, who'd noticed that I was looking a bit overwhelmed and had suggested that Cal take us back to his house for the evening. Chelsea had organized for us to stay with Cal and Milena at their new house just outside of town in the trees. Almost as soon as we walked through the doors and were met with nothing but silence, I had started to feel better.

"Are you exhausted, sis?" Cal raised an eyebrow at me. "Or maybe do you want to decompress a little?"

I looked between Cal and Cole. "I'm going to head to bed." Cole smiled knowingly. He'd been so supportive all day. It was as if he just knew when I needed him to be close and when I needed him to give me space. I owed him a huge thank-you.

"I think maybe I could use a small glass of wine," I said to Cal. "If you're okay?"

Cole laughed. "I'm good. It's been a big day." He kissed me on the nose. "Go catch up with your brother."

"Come with me, Cole. I'll show you the guest room." Milena waved in the direction of the hall, and after one more quick kiss goodnight, they disappeared.

As Cal got me settled on the couch, I couldn't help but wonder whether maybe Cole regretted his decision to come with me to Cedar Springs after all. My family was intense.

Of course, Cole didn't seem to be the kind of guy who would bother hiding his feelings about a situation. He'd tell me exactly how he was feeling and whether it was all too much for him. At least I hoped he would. There was still a lot the two of us didn't know about each other.

But I wasn't going to worry about that for the moment. Milena, sensing that Cal and I could use a little time to catch up, had opened a bottle of wine, brought us two glasses, and had excused herself to bed as well.

"I didn't mean to scare her away," I said after she'd gone.

Cal laughed. "Nothing can scare my girl. Trust me on that. If the paparazzi didn't make her run for the hills when we first met, nothing can chase her away. Especially not my big sister."

"Watch it, mister. I'm not that big." I laughed. It was easy to be with Cal. Even after all the time we'd spent apart, it was as if no time had passed at all. "But I do like her." I nodded at the door Milena had escaped through. "She's sweet. But tough. Perfect for you."

"She is." Cal's eyes took on a faraway look, and I couldn't help but smile at the sweetness. I never thought I'd see the day Cal would fall in love so completely. Sure, he'd had girls all over him in high school, and pretty much constantly since then, but none of them, including his highly publicized relationship with Australian actress Bridget Murphy, were anything like this. "I'm a pretty lucky man."

"You are." I looked around. "I mean, you all are. And for all of you to end up in Cedar Springs of all places, it's all pretty incredible."

"You're telling me." Cal laughed and sipped his wine. "I'll be totally honest, I never would have imagined myself picking a small town to settle down in. But when the opportunity to play Mr. Summer, especially when he's my own brother in real life, came up, there was no way I could say no."

Mr. Summer was the hottest new television series that was based on Gwen's super-popular social media accounts and her real-life relationship with our oldest brother, Ian. There'd been all sorts of drama surrounding the series as it was getting started, but once the filming started, and the first few episodes debuted, the drama disappeared, replaced completely by success, and the show had taken off.

"It doesn't look like you'll have to look for work anytime soon," I said. "The show is doing incredibly."

"Filming it right here is even more incredible," Cal said, ever humble. "Milena loves it here, too. And since I love her… well…it makes the decision to stay an easy one." He waved his hand. "But that's enough about me. Tell me everything about you. What has been going on?"

It had been the conversation I had been able to avoid for most of the night, considering there was so much catching up to do with everyone else. It's not that I didn't want to talk about myself—it was more that I didn't know what to say.

I shrugged and turned my attention to my glass. I swirled the deep-red liquid around and around.

"What's going on, Amber?" Cal's voice softened.

"There's nothing going on." That was the truth. Ever since I'd called Wallace and McKwade and turned down the job, there hadn't been much going on at all. Thinking of the phone call I'd made and the way I'd thanked Joshua for the opportunity, but I had to say no to the position, still made me a little nauseous.

"Are you sure?" Joshua had asked me more than once. "It's the opportunity of a lifetime."

That wasn't entirely true, but it was a great opportunity. I knew that. I also knew I couldn't take the job. Besides, there was no way Cole would be happy in Toronto.

Not that Cole was the deciding factor in turning down the job. Not at all. But he did play a part. How could he not?

The job wasn't the right thing for me. At least not for now. Not that I knew what the right thing was for me. Was it Cole? I couldn't be sure. Not of anything. Except maybe one thing—with the utmost certainty, I knew I was falling in love with him. Maybe I was already in love with him.

But what if he didn't feel the same way? Sure, I knew he liked me. A lot. But love? That was a big leap.

I sighed deeply and looked up at my brother. "I guess I don't really know what I'm doing at all anymore."

Chapter Seventeen

COLE

"I STILL DON'T KNOW why we need to drive two hours into the forest when you're literally surrounded by trees, right here." I, dressed in thick winter clothes that had been donated by Amber's brothers, stood by the pickup truck as the others loaded axes, chainsaws, and thermoses full of what I assumed was coffee, but also really hoped contained some whisky to help warm me up, into the back.

"Because the best trees are up there." Mitch pointed toward a mountain that rose impossibly high above us.

"He's kidding," Ian said. "But the best trees are a bit of a drive."

"Besides," Declan chimed in, "and more importantly, it's tradition to go out in the woods and pick a tree."

"Whose tradition?" Lucas, Chelsea's boyfriend, asked with a laugh. "I didn't think any of you actually ever spent a Christmas in Cedar Springs before." He winked at me and shook his head. As the only other man who wasn't directly related, but dating a McCormick sister, I felt a sense of camaraderie with the man despite the fact that I'd barely spoken to him.

"True," Mitch said. "But more the reason to start the tradition now, don't you think?" He handed me a thick pair of leather work gloves and opened the back door to the truck. "Welcome to the first annual McCormick tree hunt."

I laughed and climbed into the crew cab of the truck while Cal and Mitch rode up front. Lucas, Declan, Ian, and Declan's stepson-to-be, Jonah, hopped in the truck behind us, and in their own little convoy, we headed up the snow-covered mountain road.

We'd only been driving a few minutes when Cal turned around in his seat and smiled at me. "So, Amber tells me you've been living in Australia for the last few years."

There was nothing particularly antagonistic about Cal's question, but I couldn't help but feel as if I were being interrogated. "That's right."

"I was in Australia myself."

I knew that. Everyone knew that. Cal was a rising star in Hollywood. "I doubt our paths would have crossed. I was mostly in the Outback, working on ranches."

Cal nodded knowingly. "And now?"

I raised an eyebrow in question and maybe the slightest bit of challenge. "Now I'm here."

The other man smirked and turned back to face front, but only for a moment before he turned around again. "I'm not sure about you yet." Whatever I expected him to say, it wasn't that. I bristled and readied to rebut, but Cal continued. "My sister likes you, so I like that." He grinned, softening his interrogation a little bit. "But she's different with you. Really different."

"Cal, I don't—"

"Hey." Cal held up his hand, interrupting me. "Amber's my sister, and it's my job to make sure she's okay."

"I get it."

Cal tipped his head in question.

"I have a little sister myself," I said. "Josie. She used to be Amber's college roommate."

A slow smile spread across Cal's face as he took in the information. "Okay," he finally said with a broad grin. "So you know exactly what I'm saying. Good."

"I do." It was mostly a lie. I had never behaved in any kind of irrational way toward any guy Josie had brought home. I probably shouldn't have been surprised that with four brothers, there'd be some protective behavior toward me, but I hadn't expected it so soon into our visit. Still, I returned Cal's smile until the other man turned around and looked out the windshield again.

I dropped my head and shook it briefly. When I looked up, my eyes met Mitch's in the rearview mirror. For a moment, I was sure Mitch was going to take his turn grilling me. But when Mitch spoke, it had nothing to do with Amber.

"Have you ever cut down a Christmas tree before, Cole?"

AMBER

"I'M SO glad you're here." Chelsea tucked my arm through hers and skipped with me down the street. "I can't remember the last time we went Christmas shopping together."

I laughed. "I don't think we've ever gone Christmas shopping together. You hate shopping with me, remember?"

When Chelsea had shown up earlier that day and all but insisted that I go shopping with her, I'd thought it was strange, given my history of shopping together, historically an event that resulted in one or both of us frustrated and close to tears. My style was to get in and out as quickly as possible, while Chelsea preferred more of an all-day browsing approach that always threatened to do my head in.

Hesitant, but excited to spend time with my sister, I'd said yes.

"It's not that I hate shopping with you."

I looked sideways at my little sister, who laughed.

"Okay, okay," Chelsea admitted. "I kind of hate shopping with you. At least I used to. You don't like to browse, and where's the fun in that?"

"Shopping isn't supposed to be fun. You're supposed to go in, get what you need, and leave. It's just a chore to be done. Make a list, cross it off and…" I trailed off as I realized that I sounded just like the old Amber. The boring and predictable Amber. "Wait…" I risked a glance at Chelsea, who was trying not to laugh.

"It is supposed to be fun, Amber." I shook my head. "At least, it can be. Honestly. It's not always about getting a job done, making a list, and checking it twice. I mean, you're not Santa or anything." I rolled my eyes, but Chelsea didn't seem to notice. "Sometimes it's about browsing and searching for just the right item for that person you love. Or, even better, trying on a bunch of things until you discover something incredible."

"Incredible?" I raised an eyebrow, unconvinced that there was anything incredible at all about shopping.

"Yes, incredible." Chelsea stopped walking in the middle of the sidewalk and spun around so she faced me. "Haven't you ever taken something off the rack, something you never would normally try, and then when you put it on…" I spun on the snowy sidewalk as if I were wearing a ball gown and not a parka. "It's magic?"

I blinked and shook my head before answering. "Honestly?"

"No." Chelsea laughed. "Don't answer that. I already know the answer."

I couldn't help but laugh. I'd missed Chelsea's dramatic antics. Everything about her was the complete opposite of my orderly-must-have-a-plan personality.

"Oh, Chels. I missed you." Spontaneously, I pulled her into a hug and squeezed. Hard.

"I missed you, too." Chelsea kissed me on the cheek. "So much. And I'm so glad you decided to come for Christmas. Can you even believe this town?" I turned, one arm still around Chelsea, the other spread wide, taking in the main street. "It's like a perfect little Christmas town," Chelsea continued. "I'm absolutely loving everything about it. So much better than a big city for the holidays. It's like being in a Hallmark movie."

I laughed. It definitely was like that. "And being here, all together, it's absolutely—"

"Perfect."

I raised an eyebrow. "I still can't totally wrap my head around the fact that we're all...I don't actually know how to explain it."

"One big happy family?"

I laughed. "I guess that's one way to describe it. Does Dad know? That we're all friends after all this time? I bet he's just loving it." Despite the fact that our dad had made a horrible decision that had altered all of our lives, none of the McCormick children had fully disowned our father. We'd all gone through periods of being angry with him, but at the end of the day, he was our dad, and we loved him.

"I'm not sure he knows you're here," Chelsea said. "But I spoke with them both the other day to let them know I wasn't coming home for Christmas. Of course, I had to promise Mom that I'd bring Lucas to meet them before we went overseas.

Maybe you and Cole can come with us? Before you guys go… where are you going?"

I shrugged as a reflex. After our abrupt decision in the airport a few weeks earlier, we hadn't actually spent much time talking about the future or where we'd go after Cedar Springs. While we'd been at Josie's, my lack of a plan actually hadn't bothered me all that much. But ever since we got on the airplane, the what's next thought kept pushing its way into my thoughts. What were we going to do next? We couldn't just keep sleeping in Cal and Milena's spare room forever. Besides that, we would run out of money. I had no idea what Cole's situation was; I had some savings, but I couldn't support us both indefinitely.

Standing on the street in the cold December air, I started to sweat as all the questions I'd managed to keep at bay started demanding answers. I'd done a decent job ignoring my growing uncertainty. In fact, up until the moment I'd walked into the Grizzly Paw the day before, I'd put my feelings up to nerves at meeting Ian and Mitch. But now that the initial meeting had gone well, maybe there was more to my unsettled feelings than I'd thought.

"This is the store." Chelsea yanked on my hand, completely oblivious to the distress I found myself in, and pulled me into the shop. "Live, Love, Lake," Chelsea told me as the bells tinkled overhead, announcing our arrival. "It's Evie's store."

"Evie…"

"Declan's fiancée."

"Oh, right." I forced myself to focus on the moment. I'd met Evie the night before at the Grizzly Paw and instantly liked the sweet, soft-spoken woman. My brother clearly adored her, and it was easy to see why. She really was lovely, and I remembered Chelsea mentioning her store. "There was so much going on last night, it was hard to keep up."

"I get that." Chelsea lifted an arm in a wave as Evie called out to us. "You're going to love this place, though. And remember what I said about shopping being fun? Let's find you an amazing new dress for this new, I'm still not so sure about it, version of you."

COLE

AFTER THAT ONE moment in the truck when I wasn't sure whether Cal was getting ready to throw down and make it a full-on challenge, or whether it was just a warning of some kind, the rest of the tree hunting excursion was largely uneventful. At least in terms of any of Amber's brothers questioning my intentions with Amber.

By early afternoon, most of the men had found suitable trees for their various households, and the search was on for the McCormick family Christmas tree.

"It has to be at least nine feet," Declan announced as they slogged their way through almost knee-deep snow.

"Are you kidding?" Cal countered. "That room can handle at least twelve feet. Besides, it's got to be impressive."

"Like, really impressive," Mitch agreed.

Next to me, Lucas chuckled under his breath and shook his head. "Do you guys have a tree stand big enough for a tree that size?"

Everyone stopped in their tracks, and it was Ian who finally turned around to stare at Lucas, and then each of his brothers in turn. "Anyone have a stand?"

I tried my best to hide my chuckle, but when Lucas burst out in laughter, I gave in and joined him.

"Don't worry," Lucas said after a moment. "I can whip up something simple that will hold it."

Ian's face split into a smile. "All right then, let's find it." He clapped his gloved hands together and once again, they all set off. "It has to be perfect."

"Why does this remind me of the Griswolds in National Lampoon's Christmas Vacation? At least we brought an ax."

Declan, overhearing my comment, dropped back to my side. "Did you have big family Christmases as a kid?"

I shook my head. "Not like this. Your family—it's…"

"Don't I know it." Declan slapped me on the back. "I hope you're not too overwhelmed by it all?"

"Not at all," I answered honestly.

"Good to hear, because Amber really seems to like you. I can't remember her ever bringing a guy home before."

"Not even that Randy guy?"

Declan laughed. "Definitely not that Randy guy. Which is a good thing, from what I've heard of him." His laughter died down, and he added more seriously, "But I don't think she felt about him the way she feels about you." His words struck something deep in my gut, and I liked it. "But I have to tell you, Cole…"

After my chat with Cal, I was instantly on edge. I sucked in a deep breath, and my entire body tensed. "What's that?"

"Amber's different with you."

I released a little of the breath I was holding, but not all of it.

"Like, really different."

"I've heard that." I nodded. "But I don't think I can take all the credit for that. She did say she was trying to make a change."

"She's happy," Declan said. "And as far as I'm concerned, that's all that matters. I think that goes for all of us."

I wasn't so sure about that. I snuck a glance at Cal, but didn't bother saying anything.

"And you do seem to make her happy."

"That's all I want to do."

"There was a time not that long ago when I would have told you that Amber was only happy if she had a plan," Declan said. "But maybe that's changed, too." He laughed. "I'm not going to lie to you—I have never seen that woman without a firm grip of control on things." He shook his head. "Not even once. It doesn't seem normal."

Obviously, I knew Amber had a history of being predictable and making sure all of the details in her life were taken care of. That wasn't any kind of a secret. But maybe I didn't realize to what extent she liked to be in control. Was it really that unusual that she was flying by the seat of her pants right now? So unheard of that she didn't know what she was doing next?

Maybe it was. And if it was, how long would it last? Would she change her mind about what she wanted to do? About the job she'd turned down? About me?

I didn't have a chance to let myself think much deeper on it because a second later, one of the group announced, "There it is! That's the one!"

AMBER

"THAT'S THE ONE!"

I spun in the mirror again in an effort to assess my reflection.

Evie clapped her hands together. "Oh yes," she said. "That is absolutely the dress."

Never in my life had I worn anything like the one I had on. For most women, it probably wouldn't be considered that over the edge, but for me, it was absolutely the sexiest thing I'd ever had on my body—with the possible exception of the Little Red Riding Hood costume—let alone considering purchasing and wearing in front of other people.

"That color, Amber." Chelsea came to stand behind me. "It makes your hair look like gold. What do you call this color, Evie? Is it a royal or a peacock?"

"Definitely a peacock."

I turned to look at both of them with wonder. "There's such a thing as peacock blue?" I didn't wait for an answer before turning again and facing the mirror. I had to admit, my hair did look amazing. I'd taken to wearing it down more and more ever since I discovered that Cole liked it that way. Currently, it was spread over my shoulders and my bare back in soft, shiny waves.

It was a fitted dress made from some sort of silky, impossibly soft material that hugged me in all the right places, showcased my cleavage, and with the slit up the leg, exposed just enough bare thigh to make me a bit nervous. My usual dress was an office-appropriate conservative style, with a high neckline, and maybe even a size too big to keep from showcasing my curves too much. The exact opposite of what I was wearing.

It fit perfectly, as if it were made specifically for me, with no extra fabric at all to hide my body. Not only was I not hiding my body, but I was fully showing it off with a deep V-neckline that plunged dangerously deep into my cleavage. Evie had given me some sort of push-up bra to wear under the dress that had my breasts lifted so high, I didn't think it was possible to have so much cleavage.

"You are stunning," Evie said. "But wait. One more thing." She glanced down at my bare feet and took off out of the changing area, only to return a moment later with a pair of impossibly high heels in a shimmery silver.

"Oh, yes!"

I could have sworn that my little sister did a fist pump when Evie handed me the shoes that were, of course, in my size. The woman really was good at her job. She hadn't even asked me what my size was.

There was no way I was going to get away with not putting the shoes on, and I knew it. Using a chair for balance, I slipped them on. They fit perfectly.

One of the women gasped, and, a little bit scared of my own reflection, I slowly turned around to the mirror.

"You look like a sex goddess," Chelsea declared. "Holy shit!"

I didn't know what a sex goddess was supposed to look like, but I one hundred percent agreed with the second part of my sister's statement. "Holy shit," I repeated. I didn't even recognize the woman I looked at in the mirror.

"Is that...how did..."

"If you don't buy every single thing that you're wearing right now, then you are insane." Chelsea shook my head. "I wasn't sure I believed it before," she continued. "But you're right, Amber. You are definitely the furthest thing from boring and predictable. Not in that dress."

I looked at my reflection with new eyes. Chelsea was right. There was absolutely nothing boring about how I looked. I didn't even need to think about it. "Sold," I said. "I'll take it all."

Ten minutes later, when I was tucking my credit card back in my wallet and trying not to think about the growing balance on it with no way to pay it back, Chelsea tucked my arm through hers again. "See? I told you shopping was fun! Now, let's go buy some presents."

Chapter Eighteen

COLE

THE DAYS PASSED in a blur as Amber and I helped the rest of the McCormicks get ready for Christmas. Even I, who had never given much thought to Christmas before, couldn't help but fall under the spell of the holiday magic. A feat made easier because after that one uncomfortable moment in the truck when Cal grilled me on my intentions, Amber's brothers hadn't said one more word to me about what my intentions were when it came to their sister. I wasn't completely naive to think that they had totally accepted me, and every once in a while, I could have sworn I caught Cal watching me.

In fact, everyone seemed to have relaxed into the new family dynamic. Even Amber, who'd been nervous to see Ian and Mitch, and even more nervous to meet their mother, Maureen, seemed to have put those fears to rest.

We'd been so busy with tree decorating, shopping, and all the rest of it that I hadn't been able to get much time alone with Amber over the last few days, but that was going to change tonight. When I'd been in town the day before, I'd discovered the oversized ice rink that was shoveled out on the lake. It had been years since I'd been ice skating, but it seemed like the perfect time to try it out again.

Not that I would care what I was doing as long as it meant spending some much overdue time alone with Amber.

I squeezed her gloved hand in mine and pulled her a little closer as we made our way down Main Street.

"Isn't this the cutest town?" She tipped her head up to look at me. "I mean, Crystal Creek was cute, too. But this...it doesn't get any more Christmas card than Cedar Springs."

I couldn't argue with that. Just walking down the street filled me with a holiday spirit I'd never felt before. Twinkling lights were strung on every available pine tree. The storefronts were adorned with pine boughs, wreaths, and lights as well. Never mind the Christmas carols that seemed to be coming out of nowhere. The gently falling snow didn't hurt either.

As we approached the end of the street and the frozen lake where people were skating around a huge bonfire, the entire scene looked as if it were fresh out of a snow globe.

"This really is amazing," I said. "And I don't even love Christmas." I pulled her in for a hug and a quick kiss on the nose. "But that might be changing."

It was true. Everything was just a little bit better with Amber. Okay, a lot better. She made me feel things I'd never felt before. Like the Christmas spirit. I kissed her again, on the lips this time, and not for the first time contemplated telling her exactly how I felt. But once again, something stopped me.

Besides, there was no rush.

"Are we really going to do this?" She turned around in my arms. "I can't remember the last time I skated. It's going to be interesting."

"We don't have to—"

"Oh no! We're doing this." She laughed and grabbed my hand to pull me toward the booth where they could rent skates.

Fifteen minutes later, we were laced up and ready to go.

I took a few tentative steps on my blades. I reached back to take Amber's hand and help her steady herself, but before I had a chance, she was up and in two quick steps was on the ice, gliding away from me. I watched in awe as she did a quick, tight turn and, in two pushes, was on her way back.

When she came to a quick stop in front of me with a spray of ice and snow, I couldn't help but laugh. "I thought you said it had been ages since you did this?"

"It has," she insisted. "But I may have done some competitive figure skating when I was a teenager."

"You may have?"

She held up two fingers to indicate a small amount and gradually spread them apart. "I won gold in the provincial championships when I was fifteen."

I laughed again and took a few more tentative steps before pushing off and trying my own gentle glide. And then another, and another, until I was actually skating. I focused on putting one foot in front of the other, but was very aware of Amber gliding easily along next to me.

After a few minutes, I had the hang of it, and although I was nowhere nearly as skilled as Amber, I took her hand, and together we fell into a nice rhythm.

"So, if you were such a figure skating champion, how come I never saw you in the Olympics?" I was only half joking as I asked the question, but I noticed the way her hand tensed ever so slightly in mine. "I get the impression that you succeed at everything you do."

She didn't deny it, but simply shrugged. "When I was little, that's all I dreamed about."

"Then what happened?"

"The plan changed."

There was that word again. Plan.

"Why did it change?"

I watched her while I waited for an answer. Her hair was tied up in a braid again, only this one was loose and hung over her shoulder in a very sexy way. It was very different than the severe tight braid she sported when we'd first met. She had a knit cap tugged over her head and a scarf tied loosely around her neck. She was absolutely gorgeous.

"Everything changed when I was a teenager, and we found out the truth about our dad. Suddenly, figure skating didn't seem so important."

My heart clenched, imagining a younger Amber whose world had just imploded in the most dramatic way. To the point where she'd given up her dream of skating for a much safer, and...predictable plan.

"And that's when you decided to be an accountant?"

She nodded. "It seemed like a nice, safe path to take. Too much uncertainty in skating." Her mouth twisted up into a sad smile as we kept moving. She turned to look at me. "Everything was so out of control back then. It just seemed so important to be in control of something. Anything. And I could control that. Every single part of it. And it felt right."

I nodded and let her talk.

"If I worked hard, I got good grades. Then I got the school I wanted. The internship I wanted. The job..."

The job she turned down. For me.

"And now?" I almost hated to ask the question. But I needed to. As much as I didn't want to, we did need to talk about the future, in some capacity.

I'd tried not to think about it, but Cal's words about Amber needing a plan kept reverberating in my head. And now I knew why. What if her need for order was so deeply ingrained in her that this...this thing we were doing...us...couldn't possibly last?

The idea scared the hell out of me in a way I didn't expect.

I worked to control my breathing as I waited for her answer. Finally, she spun on her skate so she was in front of me and looked directly into my eyes. "Now?" She shrugged a little. "Now I—"

AMBER

"THERE YOU GUYS ARE!" Chelsea all but slammed into me, grabbed my arm, and spun to a stop on her skates as her boyfriend, Lucas, joined us. "I've been looking all over for you."

My words died on my lips, but I didn't miss the look on Cole's face as I turned away to greet my sister. I may not have been able to say what I needed to, but I couldn't help but feel as though he already knew what I'd been about to say.

But how could he know, when I didn't even know?

Not really.

I shook my head. I couldn't think about that now.

"Hey," I greeted my sister, holding tight so Chelsea didn't fall down. I'd never been as good on skates as she was. "We've been here all night. Were you looking for us?"

"Yes and no, I guess." She shrugged. "I just want to spend as much time together as we possibly can."

I laughed, but Lucas shook his head. "I keep telling her that it's okay to give you guys some time alone, too. But she won't listen."

"Of course I won't listen! I haven't seen my sister in ages, and when we go overseas to check on Lucas's new project, I won't see her until…well, who knows!" Chelsea spun and faced me. "And if you decide to go to Australia." She threw her arm over her face dramatically. "I'll never see you again."

I laughed and purposefully avoided meeting Cole's gaze. I hadn't missed my sister's choice of words, and I was pretty sure he hadn't either.

If you decide to go to Australia.

We hadn't discussed our next steps at all. But even without talking about it, I had felt things changing for me. The last few days of being around my family in Cedar Springs had been better than I'd ever expected. I never thought I'd be able to connect with my oldest brothers the way I had, and all of their women felt instantly like more sisters. I'd never before been able to experience the big happy family, and as messed up as their history was, it still felt good.

Really good.

"Earth to Amber?"

I blinked hard and shook my head a little. Chelsea had released my arm and stood in Lucas's embrace. She'd obviously been talking to me, but I had drifted off into my thoughts.

"Are you okay?" Cole put his arm on mine and squeezed gently. His eyes were full of concern, but I knew it wasn't just concern for the way I'd gotten momentarily lost in thought. He'd sensed the shift, too. And we still hadn't discussed what it was we were going to do after the holidays.

Was it insane that I'd given up such an amazing opportunity for a man who, by his own declaration, had never wanted to get married or settle down? Did I even have a future with a man like that? Was I making a huge mistake?

The questions that, for the most part, I'd managed to suppress bubbled to the surface all at once. My heart raced, and suddenly, despite the chilly air, I was too hot. I tugged at my scarf.

"Amber?"

I blinked hard to see Cole still watching me carefully. If I looked closely, I could almost see what I thought might be love in his eyes. But was it? He still hadn't told me how he felt. Except that he liked me. If he didn't admit his feelings to me, could I trust that he even had them? Or maybe that didn't matter? After all, I could just live moment to moment. I didn't really need any kind of declaration or promise from him. Did I? Maybe the new Amber didn't need long-term commitments or plans of any kind and could just wing it. Yes. I could wing it.

"I'm good." It wasn't entirely a lie. Because despite the confusion that swirled around inside me, growing more intense by the moment, I was good. Being in Cedar Springs felt like putting on a warm sweater, and being with Cole, despite the uncertainty…it felt right, too. I kissed Cole quickly to reassure him. "More than good."

And that's what I was going to focus on.

He slipped his arms around me and held me tight for a moment. I melted into his embrace, but only for a moment.

"Who's ready for some hot chocolate?" I asked.

"Only if we can spike it with something." Lucas grinned, and Cole nodded in agreement.

Chelsea rolled her eyes, but offered up a suggestion. "How about a Mogul Smoker over at the Paw? It's coffee and hot chocolate and just enough booze to help you really warm up."

"Sounds good to me." I linked my arm through my sister's. "Besides, I think Cole may have hit his limit for skating for one night."

COLE

THERE WAS DEFINITELY something going on with her. I could feel it, and it worried me. A lot.

Maybe her brother had been right, and the lack of certainty in her future was starting to get to her. No matter how much I wanted to put Cal's words out of my head, I couldn't seem to let them go. Especially with the odd shift that seemed to be slowly happening with her.

After sharing hot toddies with the others and making promises to touch base in the morning, because Chelsea really was determined to spend as much time with her sister as possible, I once again managed to get Amber alone.

But when I finally slipped under the sheets of the guest bed we were sharing, and snuggled up to Amber's smooth, warm back, the last thing I felt like doing was talking about the future.

I traced my finger down her arm and over her soft curves until my hand landed on her hip. I splayed my fingers wide and pulled her back into me. A moan slipped from her lips. It was the sexiest sound I'd ever heard.

"You're so beautiful, Amber." I kissed the back of her neck, and she wiggled closer to me. "Damn, woman. I lo—" The word died on my lips before I could say it out loud, and I instantly regretted it. She stiffened in my arms. I squeezed my eyes shut and silently chastised myself. I wanted to tell Amber how I felt about her. Of course I did, but not in bed. Not with her naked in my arms and my raging erection pressing into her back. That didn't feel right. It wasn't special. It wasn't... enough. Besides, I needed to be damn sure about my feelings for her. The last thing I wanted to do was say something I wasn't sure about, or worse, that I'd get wrong and make a mess of.

Never before had I been in love. I had no idea what it was supposed to feel like. Or what I was supposed to do with the emotions that bashed about inside me. And what if she didn't reciprocate? Would that change anything?

No.

I wasn't going to say a damn thing until it was the right moment.

Besides, Amber was distracted, and I didn't want whatever it was that was going on with her to affect the way she felt about me. And I knew what to do about that. "I look forward to figuring out the next step with you." It was beyond a lame thing to say, but it was also the truth. Besides, I wasn't stupid, and I was pretty sure I knew what was bothering Amber.

She turned in my arms, the sexy moaning a distant memory as she propped herself up on her elbow. "You what?"

I tried not to look disappointed because, as much as I would have preferred to make her moan all night long, there were things we needed to talk about. I pushed myself up to a sitting position. "I look forward to figuring out the next step with you." When I said it again, it sounded even more ridiculous. Like something an insurance salesman might say, and not at all something a man falling in love with a woman would say. I resisted the urge to groan out loud and stayed the course. "I mean, we did say our stop in Cedar Springs would be a good time to plan." I made sure to emphasize the word I knew she needed to hear.

If her brothers were even remotely right, Amber needed the stability of a plan. She needed to know what to do and what was happening next. No doubt that was why she was feeling so lost and acting so strangely. If a plan was what the woman needed, it would be exactly what I would give her.

She blinked in confusion a few times and propped herself up with an elbow. "You want to make a plan? You? You hate plans."

"That's not true." I laughed, but she was right. At least a little. "Besides, I know that's what you need." I reached across the space between us to touch her. "I know what you gave up to be here. To be with me. And I want to make sure I—"

"Is that what this is about?" She stiffened, and I had the distinct impression I'd said something wrong. Really wrong. "You think I gave everything up for you."

Alarm bells went off in my brain as I watched her shake her head. "No," I said quickly. "That's not what I was—"

"I gave it all up," Amber interrupted me. "But it wasn't for you." Tears pooled in her eyes, and I instantly wanted to hold her close so she wouldn't cry. "It was what I needed to do," she continued. "You were a…a bonus." She laughed weakly, but the laughter vanished as quickly as it had started.

"Amber." I shifted so I was closer to her, but still I didn't gather her up in my arms the way I wanted to. "I know that it wasn't about me." She winced but didn't say anything, so I continued. "And that's why I want you to know that I under-stand how hard this is for you." She blinked. "Not knowing what's happening next," I said quickly. Her lips curled up a little. A small sign that I took as a step in the right direction. "I mean, it probably wouldn't hurt if we thought about it a little bit, right?"

She didn't speak for a few minutes, but then she nodded, and a real smile crossed her face. "You're right. Okay. Yes. We should think about what comes next. I mean, we can't stay in Cal and Milena's guest room forever, right?"

It was then that I pulled her into my arms and held her tight. Relief washed over me. I had never been good at communicating my feelings with women. Especially women I cared about. Hell, I'd never cared about a woman the way I cared about Amber, so how could I have any practice with it at all? But that didn't matter. The only thing that mattered was that I had her in my arms and I was going to do whatever it took to keep her there.

If that meant making plans for the first time in my life,

that's what I'd do. I'd figure out the future as far as it pertained to Amber because that's what she wanted. Hell, it's what she needed.

Whether or not she admitted it.

And one thing I knew for sure was that I'd do whatever it took to give this woman what she needed.

Chapter Nineteen

AMBER

DESPITE WHAT COLE thought I needed, and what I would have expected myself was what I needed, the last thing I wanted to do was make plans for the future. At least, not until I knew how Cole really felt about me. Which was ridiculous, really, considering I'd been just as tight-lipped on my growing feelings for Cole.

Over the next few days, we both eagerly jumped into Christmas preparations with my family, and I managed to put Cole off every time he tried to bring up the topic of what would come next. Maybe if I could stall for some time, I'd have a little more clarity on how he felt about me. Because the one thing I did know was that despite my bravado and insistence that I wanted to go with the flow, when it came to Cole, it wasn't going to be that easy. It was one thing to risk a job; it was a completely different thing to risk my heart.

"Are you ready for this?" Cole squeezed my hand in his. "You look a million miles away."

I shook my head and focused on him. He was watching me with concern in his eyes as we walked toward the front door of Ian and Gwen's house. It was the day before Christmas Eve, and Ian had insisted on hosting a Christmas caroling party. It involved a karaoke machine and a songbook. Some of my siblings loved the spotlight; that much was certain. But I wasn't one of them. The last thing I wanted was anyone watching me while I tried to stay in tune, belting out "Jingle Bells."

"I'm here." I smiled and turned to him. "And I'm really glad you're here, too." I meant it. Despite the underlying questions I'd been trying not to focus on, I'd enjoyed every minute with Cole. Being with him was so easy, and so completely opposite from my relationship with Randy. He made my stomach flip, and I no longer had to question whether or not I was falling for Cole.

I'd fallen. Hard.

"I'm really glad I'm here, too." He kissed me then, right there in the middle of the street. Just like everything with Cole, it felt like magic. I could hardly believe that only a few months ago, he wasn't part of my daily life. Now, I couldn't imagine my days without him. And that scared the hell out of me.

"And I am ready for this." I gestured with my head toward the house. Tonight was the night that I was finally going to meet my half-brothers' mother for the first time. Maureen McCormick had been the most affected by her husband's betrayal all those years ago, and despite the fact that logically I knew it wasn't my fault, and Chelsea had already told me how warm and welcoming the woman was, I couldn't help but think that the woman would hate me on sight. "I got myself so worked up about Ian and Mitch, and that turned out to be all for naught. They're awesome."

Cole nodded.

"I don't know why I was so surprised. I mean, Cal and Declan have always been so...but Ian and Mitch were just so..." I laughed at myself. "I guess we've all changed quite a bit." But not that much, because my heart was still going a mile a minute at the idea of coming face-to-face with Maureen in a moment.

"It's going to be fine." Cole kissed me again and pulled me into a tight hug. "No need to be nervous."

I forced my breathing to slow as I snuggled deeper into his embrace.

"Are you two done making out yet?"

Despite the fact that we were definitely not making out, Cole and I pulled apart like teenagers caught out on the couch. I laughed when I saw Declan and Evie walking toward us.

"I'm never going to be done making out with her." Cole pulled me close again and placed one last kiss on my lips that sent a thrill right to my core.

"Yeah, yeah," Declan joked. "Save it for later. Let's get in there."

We fell into step with the other couple as I asked, "Where's Jonah tonight? He's going to miss out on all the singing."

The other woman laughed. "He's totally okay with that. He's with his dad tonight. They're having their celebration early so he can be with us tomorrow."

I didn't know much about the situation between Evie and her ex, but I'd heard that despite some rough patches, they were now in a good place as co-parents and had managed to make a difficult situation much better for Jonah.

Inside, the party had already started. The thing with a big family was that even if the guest list was limited to immediate family only, it still felt like a crowd. But in the best possible way. We'd only been inside a few minutes when a beautiful, older woman, who could only be Maureen McCormick, approached me.

My flight response kicked in. I glanced around for an escape route, but of course, there wasn't one. And even if there was one, I knew I wouldn't take it. I couldn't avoid the woman forever. Besides, there was no reason.

Except for my own nerves.

I forced myself to smile and not pull away when Maureen walked straight up and took my hands in hers, lifted them to her heart, and squeezed.

"I know this might be a little strange," Maureen said. "But it really is so nice to finally meet you."

There was so much warmth and acceptance in her voice that it took me off guard for a moment. This woman had every reason to hate my existence. I was proof of her husband's long-running infidelity. I couldn't even imagine the pain she must have gone through. Even more so, I couldn't begin to comprehend the strength it must take to be so welcoming of Chelsea and me. Instantly, I felt a connection and great admiration for my brothers' mother.

"Maureen, I..." Words escaped me, so I smiled genuinely instead. "You are...well, I'm just so glad to meet you and... well, I'm just so sorry."

"Stop." Maureen took on a stern, very motherly expression. "That's the last I want to hear of that. The past is in the past, and even so, it had nothing to do with you girls."

"I know, but—"

"I don't want to hear another word." She tipped her head and stared at me until finally I smiled and nodded. "We're family, okay?"

"Okay."

"Come," Maureen said a moment later. "I think if we sneak off to the kitchen, we might be able to get out of at least the first few songs that Ian and Gwen have planned."

Instinctively, I glanced around to see Cole already in conversation with Cal, a drink in his hand. Satisfied that he was in good hands with my brothers, I nodded and followed Maureen into the relative safety of the kitchen.

COLE

IT WASN'T that I didn't like Cal McCormick; I did. He was a good guy, and despite his high-profile career, he was remarkably down-to-earth. And if Cal hadn't been so openly antagonistic with me the first time we met, I was pretty sure we could be friends. As it was, every time I saw the other man, I felt as if I owed the other man some sort of explanation. It was the most ridiculous thing. After all, I was a grown man in an adult relationship with a woman, and I didn't owe explanations to anyone.

Except maybe Amber.

"Have you given it any more thought?" Cal said as he handed me a drink. We'd been in the house less than five minutes, and already I was bracing myself for the interrogation. Only this time, I was ready for it.

"What exactly have I given any thought to?"

I wasn't going to roll over easily.

"Whether you're good enough for my sister or not."

Damn.

I had not been expecting that. My spine stiffened, and I forced myself to take a sip of my drink before answering with a sharp retort. What I really wanted to do was tell the other man how I had actually considered our last conversation and was doing my best to give Amber exactly what she needed. But everything I'd been about to say vanished in the face of Cal's animosity. I let the icy-cold beer slide down my throat before swallowing hard and answering. "Oh, I know I'm good enough for your sister. And I also know I don't owe you any explanation to that end." Cal opened his mouth to protest, but I cut him off smoothly. "In fact, I think unless I'm in a relationship with you specifically, I don't have to tell you a damn thing." I put the glass down hard on the side table and crossed my arms.

It had been the wrong thing to say, and I knew it. But I couldn't help myself. Logically, I knew Cal was just being brotherly. I knew it wouldn't solve anything to be an asshole. Still, I couldn't stop myself.

Cal took two steps backward. His mouth opened and shut comically, but there was nothing funny about the anger I saw in his eyes.

It only took Cal a moment to recover. "Listen." Cal was obviously taking great pains to control his voice. He took a step closer to me, so we were almost chest to chest. If anyone in the room was paying us any attention at all, they would see in a flash that a family-friendly, festive party was about to take a turn.

I knew I should step back. I knew there was nothing to gain by provoking Cal. Especially when the man really did only have his sister's best interests at heart. Still, the stress of the last few days, the uncertainty of how Amber really felt for me and what she was willing to give up for me when maybe I didn't really deserve it after all, bubbled over, and in an instant, I was looking for a fight.

"My sister is my business," Cal spoke through clenched teeth. "If you think for one minute that I'm going to sit back and let you waltz in out of nowhere to ruin her life—"

"Ruin her life?" I swallowed hard. "That's what you think I'm doing?"

"Absolutely." Cal didn't miss a beat. "That's exactly what you're doing. Before you came along, she had a plan for her life. An excellent job offer and a degree that she'd been working on for years. She was literally on the edge of having everything she'd ever worked for and then…" Cal held up his hand and made an exploding action. "Gone. For you."

I shook my head despite the fact that I could only agree with everything Cal said. Not only did I agree with it, but everything Cal said had been in the back of my mind, too. Had I ruined her life? "It's not like that," I insisted, although there was far less certainty in my voice and even I could hear it.

"It's exactly like that. And I'm not going to sit around and—"

"Hey. What's going on here?" Mitch slipped himself into the impossibly small space between the two of us and looked at us each in turn. "Because it doesn't look to me like you guys are rehearsing your rendition of 'Silent Night.'"

I forced myself to take a deep breath and a step backward. "Nothing," I said. "Nothing's going on."

Mitch looked to his brother. "Is that right, Cal? It's nothing?"

For a moment, Cal looked as if he were going to disagree, just out of principle. But he pressed his lips together and nodded curtly. "It's nothing."

A sly smile slipped across Mitch's face. "Great. Then you won't mind if I borrow this one for a minute." Without waiting for an answer, he turned to me. "Come with me. I need some help bringing in firewood."

AMBER

"I KNOW this might be a little strange." Maureen addressed the elephant in the room straight away. The older woman instantly put me at ease and somehow reminded me of warm cookies.

My relationship with my own mother had always been a good one, even throughout the scandal, but although my mom had always loved me, she'd never been an overly affectionate woman and had certainly never exuded the same type of open affection that Maureen McCormick did with her sons.

"It should be strange," I said. "Shouldn't it?" I laughed as Maureen nodded. "But is it weird if I don't think that it feels strange at all?"

"No." Maureen poured me a small glass of wine. "That's not weird at all. I felt the same way about your sister. Well," she added. "Maybe not at first, if I'm being honest. But as soon as I got to know her, it didn't feel unusual at all, and the same goes for you. After all the boys have told me, I feel like I already know you."

I took a sip of my wine and settled into one of the kitchen chairs.

"I'm really glad you decided to come to Cedar Springs for Christmas," Maureen said after pouring her own glass and joining me at the table. "Did you know it'd been years since I've been back here myself?"

I shook my head. "I didn't know. Are you glad you're back?"

"Very much." The smile that crossed the older woman's face was genuine. "Watching my boys find love the way they have, well…the lake has always been a special place, and once again, it's brought my family together and more than doubled it in size." She laughed.

I laughed, too. "It does seem like a special place." I meant it. "I haven't spent much time in small towns until very recently, but I'm discovering that I like them. A lot."

It was something I'd been thinking about more and more since being in Crystal Creek with Josie. And those feelings had only intensified in the days since I'd been in Cedar Springs. Never before had I felt more at home, more...well, I didn't know what. But it just felt right. Way more right than moving to Toronto and taking a corporate job. And although I wasn't completely abandoning the idea of traveling either, more and more, I liked the idea of settling in a small town. I told Maureen as much and then went on to tell her how I'd met Cole and how things had changed so quickly for me.

"Wow." Maureen shook her head slowly and took a slow sip of her wine. "That's a lot of change, for sure. Declan told me that you were definitely the most responsible one, even more so than him, which I find hard to believe."

I laughed. As responsible as Declan was, he had always been far more adventurous than I was. It wouldn't have fazed him at all to jump on a plane with someone he'd just met.

"And how do you feel about it all?" Maureen asked.

"Honestly?"

"Of course."

I took my time to answer, and the other woman didn't rush me. "I feel okay about turning down the job. I didn't think I would," I said. "But I do. The more I think about it, the more I realize that I don't want to spend my life working at that intensity for someone else. I feel good about that."

Maureen nodded. "And the rest of it? What's next for you?"

I tried to hide my reaction by lifting my wine glass, but judging by the look on Maureen's face, I hadn't been fast enough to hide the confusion in my heart.

"Talk to me," she encouraged.

"I'm mixed," I confessed. "Not about leaving Toronto." I shook my head. "I think I'm more than ready to leave the big city behind. It never felt like home to me. In fact, Vancouver never felt like home either." I blinked a few times before looking up again. "Do you think that's strange? That I've never actually felt at home anywhere?"

"Anywhere?"

"No," I admitted. "I felt at home when we were in Crystal Creek. And, I know it's only been a few days, but..."

"You feel at home here, too?"

I nodded.

"That's not strange at all." Maureen's smile was warm. "Cedar Springs has something special."

"I don't want to leave." I blurted it before I realized what I'd said. A moment after the words left my lips, I pressed my hand to my mouth. "I don't know why I said that."

"Because you meant it."

I shook my head, but even as I denied it, I knew it was the truth. I'd said the words because I'd meant them. I didn't want to leave. Traveling did sound appealing. Being with Cole was appealing. But the more time I spent with my family, the more I wanted to stay put.

"I did," I admitted. "But I don't know what to do."

"Ian told me that one of your plans might include going to Australia with your boyfriend after the holidays. Is that the problem?"

I nodded. It was so easy to open up to this woman I didn't know. Maybe that was exactly why it was easy. Because she had no idea who I was, who I had been, or who I thought I could be. No preconceived notions at all. It was freeing to talk to someone like that, and without even realizing it, I was opening up to a whole host of feelings that had been building inside me.

"Have you told him yet?"

"Cole?"

Maureen nodded. "Have you told him how you're feeling?"

"No," I said quickly.

"Why is that?"

"Because if I do, I'll lose him." The idea came out of my

mouth so easily that it took me off guard. Is that how I really felt?

It was.

"He isn't one to settle down," I continued. "He's been avoiding that type of life ever since he was old enough to realize he would hate it. He's told me that repeatedly. If I tell him that not only is that what I want, but that I want it in a small town, I could lose him, and I think that I'm..."

I dropped my gaze and blinked hard to keep the tears at bay.

"You're what?" Maureen asked gently when I didn't finish the sentence.

"I think I'm in love with him." I'd never said the words out loud before, and despite the hurt in my heart, they brought a smile to my face.

"So, what's the problem?"

I didn't even hesitate because the problem, as Maureen had put it, had been growing in me every day. "I don't know if he feels the same way." I let the tears slide down my face.

"Sweetie, there's only one way to know for sure, isn't there?"

I nodded.

"It was supposed to be just fun and easy." I chuckled at myself. Crystal Creek and the Snow Ball seemed so long ago. "But you're right," I said after a moment. "There's only one way to know."

I took a deep breath and wiped my cheeks. I'd spent far too long living a half-life. Those days were over.

COLE

THE MINUTE we were outside in the crisp, dark night, I relaxed. I hadn't realized how tense my confrontation with Cal had really made me. But it wasn't all the other man's fault. Not at all. I had gotten as worked up as I had because I knew there was merit in what Cal had been saying. Of course, he had a reason to be concerned about his sister, because I hadn't stepped up and done or said anything for him to feel otherwise.

I followed Mitch over to the woodpile and immediately started stacking logs to pick up.

"Just one second." Mitch put his gloved hand on my arm. "I don't think there's a rush to get back in there, do you? After all, I'm in no rush for another chorus of 'Hark the Herald.'" Mitch laughed with a shake of his head. "I really have no idea what's gotten into Ian. I mean, I expect this type of thing from Gwen, but Ian? Christmas carol karaoke? Love does crazy things to a person."

Even in the dim light, I could see the way Mitch looked at me. Watched me and waited for...what exactly?

I shrugged. "I guess it does."

"Things like giving up your dream job and talking about moving halfway around the world with a man you'd just met."

Ahh, of course. I knew there was more to the late-night firewood gathering. I instantly stiffened. Dealing with Amber's overprotective brothers was starting to get a little tiresome.

"Hey," Mitch said, reading my mind. "I get it. Dating someone with four brothers must be a bit...well, much." I started to nod, but Mitch kept talking. "The thing is, when it comes to Amber...well..." He laughed to himself as if he'd told a joke. "With Chelsea, it was different, even though she's the youngest."

"Why is that?" I tried not to be defensive, especially because there was nothing confrontational about Mitch. He was just talking. Not like Cal. I took a deep breath and forced my hands to unclench from the fists they'd instinctively formed.

"I don't really know. And to be honest, as I'm sure you've already heard…Amber and I haven't been close." I nodded. That wasn't a secret, which made the big brother act even more flabbergasting. "But I've always known her. At least, I've known about her. And who she was," Mitch continued. "I think we're all finding this —meaning you"—he waved in my direction—"so difficult to wrap our heads around. Because it's so out of character for who she is."

Despite the fact that it was true, I was getting really tired of hearing it. "Look," I started. "I know that she's made some decisions that are a little out of—"

"Hey." Mitch cut me off. "Before you go all alpha on me, hear me out, okay?"

I swallowed hard, but I nodded, and Mitch continued.

"I'm okay with out of character," he said. "I'm even okay with making radical life choices that people don't expect. Hell, when you meet the right person, all the rules go out the window. I totally get that. Even if they're not saying it, every single one of us understands that perfectly." Mitch moved around the wood stack and started absentmindedly brushing the snow off the top logs.

"It wasn't just me," I said. "I mean, Amber made those changes for herself. As much as I'd love to take credit for her waking up to the fact that there is more to life than crunching numbers all day, I can't. It was all her. I just happened to be there. And moving to Australia, well…" I trailed off, because we hadn't actually discussed doing that for a while. "Well, I can't take credit for any of this. Good or bad."

Mitch nodded and was quiet for a moment before he picked up some wood. "Okay," he said after a moment. "I can understand that. But I don't think you're giving yourself enough credit."

I mimicked him and picked up a few logs of my own. "In what way?"

"I agree with you that her choices are coming from her. She's a strong woman, and I can't imagine she's one to make any major decision on a whim. But I also think that a whole lot of what's going on in her head has to do with you." He grinned. "So, my question to you is one that I think all of my brothers have wanted to ask you." Mitch paused, his hand on a log. "Do you love her?"

Whatever I thought Mitch was going to ask me, I hadn't been prepared for that. I stumbled over my words, coughed and choked, and, finally, before I could utter a word, Mitch stopped me.

"It's not me you need to answer that question for," he said. "It's Amber. I think you're a good guy, Cole. I do. And I would welcome you into our family without hesitation. But there's one thing that I would ask of you. If you don't love her, totally and completely, tell her before she makes any more life-altering decisions that may or may not have anything to do with you, okay?"

I was stunned, but the other man's words sank in and permeated my consciousness. Somehow, I managed a nod that seemed to satisfy Mitch.

"Good." He clapped his gloved hands together and scooped up the small stack of wood he'd prepared. "We should get back in there."

A moment later, I was alone in the dark, staring at the woodpile and trying to process what had just happened. Why hadn't I answered Mitch with a hell yes the moment he'd asked? More importantly, why hadn't I told Amber? After all, she was the only one who really deserved to hear how I felt.

AMBER

. . .

I TOOK a moment to make sure my eyes weren't red from the tears, and after finishing my glass of wine, we rejoined the party in the living room.

Cole and Mitch were missing, but before I could ask, Jade told me they'd gone to get firewood. I pretended not to notice the stack of wood in the basket next to the hearth and simply smiled. I did my best to avoid Declan's eye contact when he asked for volunteers to sing "Joy to the World," and moments before he pulled me up to join him, Gwen—thank God—cried mercy, and everyone abandoned the idea of singing altogether, opting instead to enjoy their cocktails and share stories.

Mitch returned alone with the firewood, but Cole still hadn't reappeared when I managed to excuse myself. It wasn't that I wasn't enjoying myself with my family, because I was. But I couldn't shake the questions that my conversation with Maureen had left me with. I grabbed my coat from the closet and slipped outside to get some fresh air.

The night was cool, but not too cold. I walked around the side of the house, where I could see the expanse of the frozen lake and the full moon reflected off the ice. There was very little light, and the stars filled the night sky. I inhaled deeply and allowed my head to drop back so I could stare at the millions of constellations above me.

What would the stars look like on the other side of the world?

The thought made me inexplicably sad, because in my heart I knew I'd never find out. I'd never stand next to Cole, looking up at the Australian night sky. Because in my heart, I knew that it wasn't fair to ask more of him than he was willing to give. He wanted a free life, and despite the changes I'd made, I knew I couldn't change that much. Nor did I want to.

The realization caused a physical ache in my chest because

I do love Cole. Letting him go would be the hardest thing I'd ever done. But it was the right thing to do because sometimes, love just couldn't be enough.

The thought filled me with sadness, but also a sense of peace because I'd made the decision that had been troubling me since we'd arrived in Cedar Springs.

I squeezed my eyes shut and released a long, deep breath as my cell phone vibrated in my pocket. Tempted to ignore it, I continued to stare at the night sky, but finally curiosity got the best of me, and I looked at the illuminated screen. And I was glad I did.

"Josie," I said into the phone. "I'm so glad to hear your voice right now."

My best friend picked up immediately on the conflict in my voice. "What's wrong? You sound…different. What's going on?"

I debated for a moment about not telling her the truth, but what was the point? Josie was my best friend, and she was going to hear about it sooner or later anyway. "I think I need to stay in Cedar Springs."

"Really?" Josie sounded surprised, but pleased. "So, it's going well with your family? That's great news."

It was. But it wasn't all great news.

"And Cole?" Josie continued. "That's a big change for him. I mean, a small town? Wow. But hey, I guess you can never underestimate—"

"He doesn't know."

"Know what?"

I took a deep breath. "He doesn't know that I've decided to stay."

There was silence on the other end while my friend processed what I'd said.

"I mean," I continued to fill the silence. "I only just made the decision myself. I haven't had a chance to tell him yet. And

I thought that maybe I'd just wait until after Christmas. After all, what's the point of creating a big—"

"Amber?"

I swallowed hard and squeezed my eyes shut, as if Josie were right in front of me. "Yes."

"What happened?" Josie asked the question quietly, but the words slammed into me. "I mean, you two seemed so happy and so determined to face what happened next together. What went…well…I mean…what happened?"

"Nothing," I answered honestly. "And everything."

"That doesn't make sense."

"But it does," I continued. "Being here in Cedar Springs makes me feel like I'm home for the first time since…well, ever. And Cole…"

"He doesn't want to stay?"

I hadn't asked. But I didn't need to. "Cole doesn't want this, Josie. He's never wanted this. I can't ask him to—"

"Why not?"

"Because, I…"

"Do you care about him, Amber?"

I nodded and then remembered Josie couldn't see me. "I do." My voice was barely more than a whisper.

"Do you love him?"

I didn't hesitate. "Yes." The word came out in a whisper. "But I can't give up on myself now, Josie," I added. "I just can't. These last few months, I've learned so much about myself. About what I want, and what I don't want out of life. I have to be true to myself."

"Of course you do," Josie said matter-of-factly. "But can I ask you a question?"

Again, I nodded before I caught myself. "Of course."

"Have you ever considered that the reason you feel at home in Cedar Springs has something to do with the man you're there with? Has it occurred to you that Cole might be your home?"

My friend's question took the air from my lungs. No. I hadn't considered that.

Tears slipped unchecked down my cheeks.

"He loves you, Amber. I've never seen my brother like he is with you. Not ever."

"I don't know if he—"

"Of course he does!" Josie was almost yelling into the phone.

I choked back a sob. It was all too much. I wanted to believe my friend's words more than anything else in the world. But it wasn't enough to hear them from Josie. I needed to hear them from Cole. And even if I did...would love be enough to keep us together?

Chapter Twenty

COLE

AFTER THE PARTY, where I'd managed to pull my thoughts together long enough to rejoin the group for a few hours before collecting Amber and escaping back to our spare bedroom where we'd made love and fallen asleep in each other's arms, I'd barely been able to sleep.

As connected as we'd been the night before, I couldn't help but feel as if something had shifted between us. Amber had seemed distracted, deep in thought, and when I'd asked her about it, she hadn't wanted to talk. Instead, she'd kissed me. As much as I loved kissing her, I couldn't help but feel as though she were using sex to distract me from whatever it was that was bothering her. It felt different. More intense.

Amber had fallen asleep tucked up against my chest and I had spent most of the next few hours stroking her hair, dropping soft kisses on her head, and pulling her even closer, as if she could slip away at any moment.

Maybe she could? I wouldn't let it happen.

I couldn't. Because without a doubt in my mind, I was in love with Amber McCormick. And the thought of losing her, or not being enough for her, scared the hell out of me. But despite that fear, I knew that the only thing worse then losing her would be losing her without fighting for her. And for a woman like Amber, fighting for her meant telling her exactly how I felt about her.

And that's exactly what I was going to do.

Which was why I'd slipped out of the bed before she'd woken up.

I hadn't needed either of the talks with Cal and Mitch for me to come to my own conclusions about how I felt about Amber, but maybe it had given the push I needed to do something about it. Either way, it didn't matter.

I'd spent far too long running away from something I thought I didn't want, but the truth was, in all my running, I hadn't known what I wanted. Maybe I hadn't known until it presented itself in the form of a gorgeous blonde with a tight French braid and a penchant for planning.

The thought of that version of Amber made my lips curl up into a smile as I walked down the main street of Cedar Springs right before I stopped in front of the store I'd been looking for.

This was it. I knew what I needed to do. More than that, what I wanted to do. It would be a huge leap for me. But I was ready. More than ready.

Especially if it meant I got to be with Amber.

With a huge grin on my face, I pulled open the door of Live, Love, Lake and stepped inside to buy Amber a Christmas present.

AMBER

I HAD BARELY SEEN Cole all day. He'd said something about doing some last-minute Christmas shopping when I'd texted him earlier, but he'd promised to be back in plenty of time to go up to the Springs resort for the big Christmas Eve party that was happening that night.

The Springs hotel was an exclusive spa resort that had been a boon to the economy of Cedar Springs since it had opened only a few years earlier. And, of course, being the small town that it was, my siblings had all become friends with many of the locals who both worked there and owned it.

The resort was hosting a big party, and although I would have been happy with a quiet Christmas Eve spent watching holiday movies and drinking eggnog, I was looking forward to an excuse to wear my new dress.

All day, I'd tried not to think of the decision I'd already made, focusing instead on being with my family and enjoying what was the first big holiday together with all my siblings. There'd be plenty of time to get Cole alone and have the conversation I'd been dreading. But that could come later. Much later.

There was no need to ruin Christmas.

And that's what I was still telling myself as I walked into the ballroom of the Springs resort with Cal and Milena hours later. I'd spent a little extra time on my hair, and Jade had helped me with my makeup, since my skills in that area were pretty much nonexistent. The peacock-blue dress we'd picked out earlier in the week showed off every curve I had, and even some I didn't know I had. Paired with the shoes Chelsea and Evie had convinced me to buy, I had to admit, the entire effect was amazing.

When I looked in the mirror, I could hardly believe that I was the woman staring back at me.

"You seriously look fantastic," Milena said for the dozenth time that night. "Cal, doesn't she look incredible?" It was a question she'd asked him at least as many times.

My brother grunted begrudgingly, but he smiled. "You really do look stunning, Amber. Really." I kissed him on the cheek. "Cole won't even know what hit him. Where is he, anyway? I haven't seen him all day." He made a show of looking around the room.

I tried not to look bothered by the fact that I'd really wanted Cole to accompany me to the party that night. I'd been a little upset when he'd texted to say that he'd meet me there, but I'd squashed the feelings.

After all, I had no right to demand anything of him. And I needed to keep reminding myself of that.

"I'm sure he'll be here shortly."

But even after we got drinks and Cal introduced me to a few of the locals he knew from town, Cole still hadn't shown up. I forced myself not to look at my phone. After all, if he didn't want to be there, I would have my answer about how he felt about me, and I wouldn't even have to ask.

I kept the smile I didn't completely feel pasted to my face, but when the beginning strains of a familiar song filled the air, I no longer could hold back my feelings. As quickly and subtly as I could, I excused myself from the conversation with people whose names I didn't remember anyway, and started to make a beeline for the washroom. Maybe I could hide there until the song was over.

I hadn't quite made it to the safety of the restroom when the lyrics of the Thomas Rhett song I'd been trying to avoid reached my ears. It had only been such a short time ago that I'd danced with Cole to these words at the Snow Ball. Only a few weeks ago, when he'd held me in his arms and for the first time in my life I'd felt safe and wanted and needed. And now…

Tears threatened, but I was determined not to ruin my makeup. I increased my pace because I couldn't listen to even one more note, not without bursting into tears—which was something I really didn't want to do. Not in front of everyone. No. I had to get out of there. I almost made it when I felt a hand on my arm.

I spun around, ready to tell whomever it was that there was an emergency and I really had to go. But it was Cole who stood there.

In an instant, the air was sucked from the room.

"You look…" Cole shook his head and sucked on his bottom lip for just a moment before trying again. "You look absolutely ravishing, Amber. May I have this dance?"

COLE

SHE WAS the most beautiful woman I'd ever seen in my life. Not that I needed any more reason to say what I needed to say, but with only one look at her, I knew it in my heart.

She was unequivocally the woman of my dreams.

I led her to the dance floor and pulled her close into my arms. The downside to that was that I could no longer admire how gorgeous she was. The upside, of course, was having her pressed close to me. A feeling I never wanted to let go of.

We moved easily for a few beats, letting the lyrics wash over us. But then it was time. I couldn't hold it in a moment longer.

"Amber, I need to tell you something."

Instantly, I regretted my choice of words as she stiffened in my arms. But I couldn't stop, not for anything. "It's something I should have told you earlier, but—"

"It's okay." She cut me off and tried to wiggle out of my grip. In response, I tried again to pull her close. "I knew it was coming."

"You knew what?" Something was wrong. Her body language changed in an instant. Come to think of it, she'd been tense from the moment we got on the dance floor. And when I'd caught up to her outside of the restroom, had she been trying to leave?

Something was very wrong.

"Amber, what's going on?" I stopped her to look in her eyes. "I need to tell you that—"

"I know." She interrupted me again. "I know it's not going to work. I know you need to keep moving, and I'm not sure I can go." She shook her head. "No. That's not true. I know I can't go. Not permanently, anyway. I need to be here. I need to be close to my family. And I know you aren't the type to settle down and have a relationship. You told me so, and even though I said it was okay, it's not. Because I need more. I want more. And as much as I want you to want it too, I know you don't, and that's okay. I mean, it's not okay. Nothing about it is okay because I love you, and I wish it could be different. But I totally understand, and I guess what I'm trying to say is that it's okay and you don't have to say anything because I think I already knew, so you're off the hook."

She wasn't crying, but the unshed tears shone in her eyes, ready to spill over. Except they wouldn't. I knew her well enough to know that she wouldn't cry until she was alone. But I'd be damned if I was going to allow that to happen.

Especially after a speech like that. When I was sure she was done with her ranting ramble, I shook my head. "Are you finished?"

She nodded and pressed her lips together. They had a

swipe of light-pink lip gloss on them and looked so completely kissable, but I forced myself to focus.

"Good," I said.

We'd stopped dancing while Amber spewed forth the verbal barrage she'd obviously been holding back for a while. But I once again took her in my arms and led her to the beat of the song I'd forever think of as ours. The one I'd specifically asked the DJ to play. I spun her gently, but didn't release her from my grip. When she came back and once more was pressed up against me, I whispered in her ear. "I love you, too. Very much. I was hoping to say it first, but you kind of beat me to it."

I heard her breath hitch, but I wasn't done. Not by a long shot.

"In fact," I continued, "I've loved you for some time now. I just didn't know how to say it, and to be totally honest, I was a little bit scared you wouldn't say it back. Or if you did, that I wouldn't be enough for you."

She started to say something in protest, but I still had more to say. I cut her off smoothly and continued. "But then I realized that if I never told you how I felt, I could lose you forever, and that wasn't something I was willing to risk. Because the truth is, Amber, I've never felt the way I feel about you. Not even close. And maybe there was a time when I thought I'd never be a relationship guy, but that was before you. Before this." I pulled back a little then so I could look her in the eyes.

The blue of her dress made her eyes sparkle.

"I know it hasn't been long, but I don't think there's any kind of time limit on these things, and I hope you feel the same way. Because the truth is…"

I took my hand from the small of her waist and dug into the pocket of my suit jacket before I produced the ring I'd bought from Evie's store earlier in the day. Without releasing her other hand, I dropped to my knee in front of the love of my life. There was a room full of people with their eyes on us, but I didn't care. I only had eyes for Amber.

"I love you, Amber McCormick, and if you'll have me, I would love to spend the rest of my life making plans and going on adventures with you. From the moment you sat on me on that couch at Josie's house, I knew. Spending a life with you is all I'll ever need, and I hope with all of my heart that you feel the same way." I held out the vintage diamond ring. "Will you go on the greatest adventure of our lives and marry me?"

She stared at me; her mouth fell open, but still she didn't say anything. I became very aware of the way the music had stopped, and the room had grown very quiet as the crowd waited for her answer.

The moments seemed to tick by in slow motion, but finally Amber said, "Really?"

I nodded. "Really."

"You're sure?" She shook her head, and a tear finally slipped free and down her cheek. "But I just told you that I want to stay, and I know you need to—"

"I need you."

"But Cedar Springs?"

"Absolutely."

"A small town? Settling down? All of it… you're—"

"All in, Amber. All. In."

Around us, I began to register some whispers. Amber didn't answer me. She shook her head a little, but after a moment, a smile started to cross her face, so I asked again.

"Amber McCormick, whatever it is that life throws at us: small towns, world travel, kids, family, career changes, sickness, health…all of it. I want to face it with you." I swallowed hard and, still on my knee, said, "Will you marry me?"

Still, she waited a beat. But finally, the one word I'd been dying to hear came out of her mouth. "Yes."

I jumped to my feet and pulled her into my arms. I pressed

my lips to her beautiful mouth and kissed her deeply as if our lives depended on it.

Around us, the crowd cheered and let out a series of hoots and hollers, but I was barely listening. I took the ring that I still held in my fingers and slid it on her finger before pressing a kiss to it and looking up to meet her gaze again. "Whatever it is you need from me, Amber…I want to be that guy. If you need to make plans and figure things out, I'll do it. If you want to go on adventures and travel, let's do it."

She closed her eyes for a moment. "I want it all," she said after a moment. "But maybe, we could make Cedar Springs a bit of a home base?"

I looked over her shoulder for the first time and saw her entire family standing by with smiles on their faces and tears in their eyes. I let my gaze travel over to where Cal stood with Milena. She had her hands clasped and held up to her mouth, but it was Cal I focused on. I wasn't sure what I'd see in the other man, but when we locked eyes, Cal nodded…and smiled.

I couldn't help but laugh as I looked back at Amber. "I think maybe we could do that. It looks like your brothers might just accept me yet."

Amber's face screwed up in question, but before she could ask what I was talking about, I kissed her again.

"This is our perfect moment." Her smile lit her up. "I love you, Cole."

My heart flipped. If I heard those words a million times, it still wouldn't be enough.

"Merry Christmas, my love." The music had started up again, and because I wasn't ready to share her yet, I pulled her back into my arms and twirled her once more around the dance floor.

Epilogue

NEW YEAR'S EVE

AMBER

"Really? You want me to find you a house?" Milena all but jumped up and down, her excitement clear. "You're staying? For real?"

I laughed and gave my new friend a hug. The two women had become fast friends in the short time that Cole and I had been in Cedar Springs. I had very much enjoyed the time we'd spent together living in Cal and Milena's house, but it was time to move on.

Especially if we were going to be staying.

And we were going to be staying.

Cole's proposal had been the most amazing, unexpected, and romantic thing that had ever happened to me. It wasn't until the day after Christmas that we'd had a chance to sit down together and properly discuss what sharing a life together was going to look like. To my surprise, and complete joy, our thoughts weren't too far off, but the biggest similarity was also the most important—as long as we were together, we'd make anything work.

"We are going to stay," I said as together we surveyed the living room of Cal and Milena's house, where the New Year's party was to be held. "But we can't afford much," I added quickly. "At least not yet."

"I think it's so exciting," Milena said again. "You are going to love it here. I just know it."

"I already love it. Besides, I had no idea this town was in such desperate need of an accountant." It hadn't taken me long to discover that with only one local accountant in town, and a growing economy with more and more businesses opening every day, my skills were in high demand. There was a lot to do to prepare, but as soon as the New Year's celebrations were over, I planned to take the necessary steps to start up my own business. For the first time in a very long time, I was excited about working. I knew it would take a lot of effort, but Cole was on board, and it wasn't as if I'd be working myself to the bone for a giant corporation this time; it was for myself. And that made all the difference in the world.

"Thank goodness you're setting up shop." Milena handed me a party hat before selecting one for herself. "You're going to be turning away business, for sure. And what about Cole? Has he decided what to do?"

"I absolutely have." Cole appeared and slid one arm around my waist. He pulled me close and pressed a kiss to my cheek. "I'm going to offer tours." He grinned.

"Tours?"

"Snowmobiles in the winter and ATVs in the summer," Cole explained. "I'll start out small and hopefully be able to expand in no time."

"I actually think that's a great idea. This town is booming in a way I've never seen before, and I bet the tourists will love something like that."

"That's our hope."

Cole squeezed me tighter, and I all but melted against him. Everything was happening so quickly, but it was happening. We had a lot of plans, but a lot of things were still up in the air, and as unusual as that was for me, I actually kind of liked it. Because as long as Cole was my constant, I would be fine.

It was funny how much things could change.

"Are you guys ready out here?" Cal appeared in the door to the kitchen and held a bottle of wine aloft. "I thought we could have a glass of wine before everyone got here."

"Too late!" We all turned toward the front door, and Declan, who stood in a small crowd with the rest of the McCormick clan. "Let's get this party started."

COLE

"I'd like to make a toast."

The entire room fell quiet, which was quite a feat for the McCormick clan. I instinctively slipped my arm around Amber. Any excuse to hold her close. I snuck her a kiss before turning to look at Maureen McCormick, the matriarch of the family, who'd raised a glass of champagne.

"Just before we ring in the new year," she said. "I wanted to propose a toast to you all. My sons…" She looked at each of the boys in turn, giving them all a little smile. "And you girls, too. I know it hasn't been easy, but you two also feel like family to me." She pressed a hand to her chest. "It's incredible that in such a short time I can love you both as if you were my own."

Next to me, I heard Amber sniff back a tear. I knew she felt the same.

"It makes a mother's heart happy," Maureen continued, "to see her children find love the way you all have. Our family has expanded in all the best ways, and I just wanted to take a moment to toast to the future that I'm sure will be filled with just as much love and excitement as today." She raised her glass high, and we all followed suit.

"To the—"

"What about you, Mom?"

Maureen's face registered shock as Declan's words hit her. She recovered quickly, but I didn't miss the flash of pain that crossed her features.

She lowered her glass and looked to her son. "I think sometimes when you hit a certain age, you don't worry about those things anymore."

I didn't know Maureen very well yet, but even I didn't believe the words that came out of her mouth. She was a woman with a lot of love to give, and she hadn't been given a fair deal in life. No one should experience the type of heartbreak and betrayal she had.

"You know that's not true," Declan challenged her.

Beside me, Cal joined his brother and stood by his side. "It's your turn, Mom."

"It's way past your turn," Ian said from across the room. He, too, went to join his brothers.

It was then that Maureen started to look around. Her eyes landed on Mitch.

He grinned. "They're right, Mom." He left Jade's side and joined his brothers. "Which is why we got you a little something."

Her mouth formed a perfect O, and she quickly raised her hand to cover it. "Oh, no." She shook her head. "I meant what I said—my time has passed."

I looked down at Amber, but she looked just as surprised as Maureen did. Whatever it was that was going on, it was between the McCormick brothers. The sisters didn't know anything at all.

Declan stepped forward then and handed their mother an envelope. "I'm sorry it's a little late, Mom. But we wanted to get you a little something."

"You don't have to open it now," Mitch added quickly.

"In fact," Ian jumped in. "Maybe wait until you're alone."

"And ready." Cal smiled.

"Ready for what?" Maureen's voice was shaky, but she took the envelope from Declan's outstretched hand.

"For love, Mom," he answered simply. "You deserve it."

He pulled his mother into a hug then, and the other men joined in.

"What's that all about?" I asked Amber, but she only shook her head and looked to Chelsea.

Chelsea smiled from across the room and quickly made her way over. "It turns out that Maureen was in love before Dad," she started to explain quickly and in a hushed voice, although we appeared to be the only two people in the room who had no idea what was happening. "He was the love of her life, but she didn't go with him when she had the chance. Something she always regretted. I think Declan finally tracked him down. His name is Adam. Anyway, Declan reached out, and I think Adam wrote her a letter."

"No way!" Amber looked from her sister to Maureen, who was once again holding her glass of champagne, albeit this time with a slight shake to her hand. "That's so romantic."

It was. And judging by the look on the older woman's face, she thought so too.

"It's almost time to countdown!" someone across the room called out, breaking the intensity of the moment. Someone else clinked on a glass, and then everyone was counting.

10...

Evie moved around quickly and topped up everyone's glasses with champagne.

9...

I slipped my hand into Amber's and squeezed.

8...

She looked up and smiled at me.

7...

"I love you."

6...

She laughed and said it back. I'd never grow tired of hearing it.

5...

We turned our attention to the oversized television screen where the ball drop was being broadcast.

4...

I snuck another look at Amber, her blonde hair in waves over her shoulders.

3...

She was the most beautiful woman in the world. And she was mine.

2...

She turned to look at me, and our eyes locked.

"Happy New Year!"

The room broke out in shouts and whistles and noise of all kinds, but I ignored them all because the only thing that mattered was the woman who stood before me. With my free hand, I cupped Amber's cheek and pulled her in for a deep kiss, and rang in the new year and our future.

***

Find out what Maureen's letter says in the McCormick Series Finale. It's time that the matriarch gets her own happy ending in Our Forever Moment, next!

Read a special excerpt next.

And if you want even more romance...click <u>HERE</u> for an exclusive FREE novella that isn't available anywhere else!

Our Forever Moment

PRESENT

PLEASE ENJOY *this excerpt from Our Forever Moment.*

MAUREEN

Present

Crows' feet. Laugh lines. *Salt-and-pepper* strands.

Such silly names meant to soften the blow of getting older.

All they did was make me shake my head. Or sigh. It depended on the day.

Today, I sighed.

I took one last look in the mirror and tried to stifle my groan. Maybe a facial or one of those peels that the younger girls were always going on about might have helped. But it was too late for that now. The reflection in the mirror was going to have to do.

Lines, wrinkles, spots, and all.

Never in all my fifty-six years had I given much thought to

aging. I'd never been one to spend hundreds of dollars on fancy creams, or worry about dyeing the gray away. I'd always considered myself a fairly attractive woman, even as time began to take its toll.

But this was different.

Very different.

I hadn't seen Adam since I was a girl.

Yes. It was *very* different.

I reached for the makeup bag Jade, my daughter-in-law, had helped me pack just for the occasion. At my request, Jade, who had a lot more experience with this type of thing, had helped me pick out a few flattering shades of eyeshadow and even a new lipstick.

I pulled out the tube of lipstick and leaned in close to the mirror. If there ever was going to be a time to try it out, it might as well be now. After all, what else did I have to lose? My sons—most of them, anyway—thought I was crazy, traveling across the continent to a remote mountain inn in the North Carolina Mountains, only a few days before Christmas to meet a man who was a virtual stranger.

And maybe I was.

I laughed at myself as I pressed the tube to my lip. Right as my hotel room plunged into darkness.

My breath caught in my throat and panic gripped me.

"Calm down, Maureen." My voice was loud in the dark, empty room. "It's just a power outage." I laughed at myself and shook my head. I'd lived through many power outages over the years. Especially as a girl when I spent my summers in the mountainous town of Cedar Springs. Besides, I was a grown woman. There was nothing to be scared of.

Still. It *was* dark.

I'd arrived at the inn earlier in the afternoon, and even before the sun went down, it was dark and gloomy outside as the storm that had been threatening started to make good on its threats. It wasn't yet dinnertime, but with the thick storm clouds blocking out what little sunlight there might be left, my room was shockingly dark. And when, after a few minutes, the power didn't return, I fumbled for my purse and made my way out of the room and down to the main lobby of the inn.

I made the right choice. Candles were lit among the pine boughs that seemed to be draped on every free surface for the Christmas season. And paired with the welcoming glow from the huge fireplace, it was easy to forget that there was a power outage at all since the scene was so festive.

"Not to worry, Mrs. McCormick." Lucy Gibbons, the innkeeper who'd greeted me earlier, appeared beside me. She set a light hand on my shoulder. "It's not unusual for the power to go out in such a heavy storm, but we do have backup generators, and they should be up and going any minute now."

"Oh, I'm not worried." I smiled warmly and let my gaze drift around the room. "It's absolutely beautiful in here."

The woman beamed with pride. "Christmas is my favorite holiday and there's nothing quite as romantic as the festive season in the mountains, is there?" She winked, and I blushed despite the fact that Lucy couldn't have known why I was in North Carolina at the Merry Falls Inn less than a week before Christmas, or who I was meeting. "And now, with the snow coming down so heavily, it looks as if we'll be snowed in."

"Snowed in?" I turned my head around to face her. "The road is closed?"

Lucy nodded. "I just got word. The mountains are so unpredictable and although it doesn't happen terribly often, it does happen that sometimes the plows just can't keep up and—"

"But if the road is closed…" *Would Adam be able to get through?* I didn't finish the thought aloud.

"Not to worry, Mrs. McCormick. They'll have them cleared before Christmas."

Christmas? I hadn't even thought of that. My boys would kill me if I wasn't back in time for the holidays. They really wouldn't be happy if I was trapped.

But that wasn't my primary concern at the moment.

If Adam couldn't make it, after all these years and all our careful planning…well, I didn't want to think about the idea that my sons had been right, and it was a foolish idea coming so far for a man I hadn't seen in almost forty years.

Most of my sons. Declan had not only been supportive but had taken it upon himself to locate Adam as a special Christmas surprise a year earlier. I'd dedicated my life to my boys and after my husband's betrayal, when my eldest was only eighteen, I had shut my heart off to the idea of ever loving again.

But time had a way of softening things. And after I'd witnessed the way each of my sons had found their partners and a happiness I'd never seen in them before, I couldn't help but start to believe that maybe love might exist after all. And then, when my *daughters*, who really weren't my daughters at all, but my sons' half-sisters—a complicated relationship if ever there was one—also found their happiness, I was convinced that it wasn't necessarily too late.

I looked around the festive inn. *Maybe Adam had made it? Maybe it wasn't too late after all.*

"What about tonight?" I reached a hand out and stopped the busy innkeeper before she could run off. "Will anyone be able to get through the roads tonight?"

The look on the other woman's face told me everything I needed to know, but it wasn't until Lucy shook her head that my heart fell.

"With a heavy snowfall like this, it can be pretty dangerous on those mountain roads. If anyone was out there, they probably would have been turned around before they closed the gates. But—"

"Ms. Gibbons?" A rather frazzled-looking young man tapped on the innkeeper's shoulder and shot me an apologetic look. "I really am sorry to interrupt," he said. "But there's a bit of a…" He leaned in and tried to whisper. "Situation."

"A situation?"

"Is everything okay?" I straightened my shoulders and immediately went into problem-solving mode. As a mother of four boys, it was a mode I was proficient in. "If there's anything I can do, please let me know. I can—"

"Oh no." Lucy offered me a warm smile. "Everything is just fine. And like I said, the backup power should be on any moment now. There's fresh coffee, tea, or hot chocolate over by the fire. The restaurant is open and the bar next door is also available for meals and, of course, libations to get you through the cold night. The band will be—"

"The Lost Ridge Ramblers are great," the young man interjected.

"They really are." Lucy nodded. "It should all be quite festive and fun."

"It does sound fun." The innkeeper was busy, and I didn't want to add to her stress by inquiring about Adam's arrival status. I glanced out a nearby window into the snowy night and the quickly accumulating drifts, and sighed.

I didn't need anyone to tell me what I already knew.

Adam wasn't coming.

"Don't let me keep you." I forced a smile. "I think I'll help myself to a tea and sit by the fire for a while. It's really quite beautiful in here."

Lucy beamed. "Thank you. We take pride in our holiday decorations."

"It shows." I made my way to the beverage cart where, instead of the tea, I opted for a hot chocolate with marshmallows in it. I probably wouldn't be able to sleep due to the sugar, but given the storm, sleep was likely off the table anyway.

Two inviting chairs were set in front of the fireplace. One was occupied by an elderly lady working on a crochet project. The other was free.

"Is this seat taken?"

The woman looked up from her project and tipped her head. "It is now." She nodded toward the chair and set the crochet project down in her lap. "Is that hot chocolate you're drinking?"

"It is." I looked from my hot drink to the woman. "Would you like a cup?"

"With extra marshmallows, if you don't mind."

I grinned. "I'll be right back."

I returned a moment later with a mug for my new friend, complete with the requested extra marshmallows.

"Don't tell my niece." The woman winked as she accepted the cup. "She means well, but she's very bossy."

A small chuckle slipped from me as I took my seat. "I have the same problem with my sons. They're not too bad, yet," I added quickly with a shake of my head. "But if they knew about this storm…well, I can't even imagine what they'd say. They didn't like me coming so close to Christmas as it was."

"Well, what they don't know won't hurt them, will it?" The older woman lifted her mug in a toast. "My name is Elise, and I don't think there's anything wrong with keeping a few harmless secrets from our children."

"It's very nice to meet you, Elise. I'm Maureen." I grinned over the rim of my cup. "And I couldn't agree more."

I HAD KEPT MORE than my share of secrets from my children over the years. It was what mothers did. But only when it really mattered. For example, children had no business knowing the sins of their father. It was the mother's job to protect her children. And that's exactly what I'd done. For as long as I could.

Despite what others thought, I'd long known about Harold's affair and the children borne from it. I'd never forget the day I'd discovered the photograph in his briefcase of the two little girls. They looked to be about the same ages as my two youngest boys, Declan and Cal, and I'd known at once exactly what it meant. The girls shared the same beautiful eyes as my own boys, along with their father's nose. There was no doubt whose children they were.

He hadn't taken great pains to hide it from me, but at the same time, he behaved as if everything were normal. Maybe I should have confronted him years earlier, but for reasons that were my own, I never could bring myself to say anything.

What would have been the point?

They had a nice marriage. Harold was a good provider. A good father. He loved me, and I loved him. It didn't matter that we weren't *in* love. In college, there'd been a time when Harold had been desperately in love with me. His pursuit was relent-less. He showered me with gifts and compliments and finally, when I'd run out of reasons to object, I found myself loving him back. It wasn't a passionate, couldn't quite breathe, love. But it was enough.

At least, I thought it was.

And it had been enough for a little while. It wasn't long after Mitch, my second son, was born that I started to notice a shift in Harold. It was also about then when I had two toddlers in tow that I'd started packing up the boys and spending summers at the lake in the house I'd frequented as a girl that my father had left me when he passed away. After a minor bout of the *baby blues* that lasted a little too long, I'd once more been drawn to the one place I'd fallen in love as a young woman.

I hadn't understood my feelings back then, not completely. But time and distance had made it perfectly clear. Cedar Springs was home. Harold was busy building his career in the city, but he found time to make the drive every weekend and join his young family in my happy place.

The mountains were healing, and I'd returned to the city in the fall rejuvenated, refreshed and pregnant with Declan.

It was also that summer that Harold had done some *healing* of his own, and unbeknownst to me at the time, found love with someone else as well.

For years, I kept the charade of a happy family. Every summer, I would retreat to the lake. It was the only place I felt complete, and—although I'd never admit it to anyone, especially myself—being at the lake connected me to a time when I'd been the happiest I'd ever been.

Harold would arrive on Friday evenings with a bottle of wine and a fresh bouquet of flowers from the greenhouse on the highway. He'd spend Saturday and Sunday with the boys on the water, pulling them behind the boat as they showed off their growing water-skiing and wakeboarding skills, or teaching them to fish. On cooler days, Harold would take the boys into the forest, where they'd hike for hours. He'd point out animal signs and show how to build shelters and make fires. He loved his boys, and he was an excellent father.

And that's why I'd stayed quiet for so many years. It was more important for Ian, Mitch, Declan, and Cal to have a father who loved them present in their lives than it was for me to have a loving or faithful husband.

If I were honest, I'd always blamed myself in a way for Harold seeking love from someone else. Certainly, I loved Harold but I'd never loved him the way I knew I should have. I'd always held back.

How could I not, when I'd already given my heart away years earlier?

"THIS IS DELICIOUS."

I was pulled from my memory and back into the moment as the woman seated across from me sipped at her drink.

"It really is." I tested my own drink and closed my eyes as the sweet, delicious chocolate coated my tongue. "Oh wow. It really is good." I opened my eyes to see Elise enjoying her drink the same way.

"Isn't it? They've always had the best hot chocolate here at Christmas. Maybe it's the spirit of the season that makes it taste so good."

"Maybe." I took another sip. "Or it could be the hint of peppermint."

Elise laughed, a sweet sound. She plucked a tiny marshmallow from the top and popped it in her mouth. "You're here on your own."

It wasn't a question, but something about the woman made me want to talk. "I'm actually supposed to be meeting someone," I said. "But I don't think he's coming,"

Elise took a long, slow sip of her drink, and when she looked up again, there was chocolate on her upper lip. "Do you have a reason to think he might stand you up?"

I did. But at the same time, I didn't.

"Are you here with your niece?" I deftly changed the subject.

The older woman laughed before leaning forward and winking conspiratorially. "She'd…how do the kids say it now? *Freak out* if she knew I was down here by myself. I told her I was going to bed, and she had some work to do. She works too much. She tried to tell me that we couldn't come this year. But I insisted."

Elise's choice of words struck me, and I, too, laughed.

"This year? Do you come here a lot?"

The older woman's face softened. "Every single year for over sixty years."

"Really? Sixty?

"Sixty-one, to be specific."

"Wow." I sat up in my seat. "That must be a record. You've been a guest here for sixty-one years?"

Elise laughed. "Well, not quite a guest. At least not always. When I was a girl, much younger than I am now, I took a job here a few years out of high school. I started out cleaning rooms." She chuckled. "It was not a glamorous job by any stretch of the imagination, but for me, it was the greatest opportunity I could have been offered."

Fascinated, I settled back in my chair, the mug warming my hands as I listened.

"You see," Elise continued, "that was back in the days when there weren't very many choices for unmarried girls. Or married ones, for that matter," she added as an afterthought. "Not unless your family had a lot of money. And mine did not. It would have been different for you. I must have at least forty years on you."

"I'll be fifty-six next year."

"Ah, I just celebrated eighty-eight. Those years make quite a difference."

I couldn't argue with that. I'd often thought of my own mother, for whom going to college had never even been an option. I was also very much aware that I'd been born to a father who was a physician and, as such, had enjoyed a certain level of privilege.

"I'd grown up poor in a little town north of here with fewer opportunities than there were people. So when I heard that

Merry Falls Inn was hiring, it felt very exotic, like an adventure. And I was more than ready for a little adventure."

I couldn't miss the sparkle in the woman's eye as she spoke about the past.

"That must have been so exciting, Elise. What an adventure, indeed. This place must have made quite an impact on you if you kept coming back for all these years."

Elise took her time looking around the lobby, a warm smile on her face as she took it all in. "I sure didn't know all those years ago how much of a mark on my life it would leave. That's for sure." She was quiet for a moment and then, as if she realized I was still there, she shook her head clear. "I fell in love."

I waited a beat. "With Merry Falls Inn? Or with someone else?"

The smile on Elise's face told me the answer, even before she spoke. "Both."

I knew that feeling well. I smiled to myself a little, gave myself a moment to pull up the memory and started to share my story.

———

Thirty-Seven Years Ago...

I was in love. Totally and completely in love. There was no other word for the way I felt. I could feel it in my bones and every breath that I took when I looked out, off the deck at the lake below. I was totally in love with Cedar Springs and the mountain lake.

My father bought the cabin when I was a child and had started taking me and my older sister to the lake for the summers, almost as long as I could remember. But what I couldn't remember was ever feeling the way I felt at that exact moment. I attributed it to the fact that I was no longer a child.

Freshly graduated from high school, and at the very mature age of eighteen, I was a woman. I looked at things differently now. With an eye of maturity. Which was why when I looked out off the deck that towered over the blue, mountain lake where I'd spent my childhood summers swimming and splashing, I saw that same view now with love in my eyes.

The footsteps on the deck boards behind me interrupted my quiet moment of reflection. A second later, my best friend Sue Ann appeared next to me. Sue Ann draped herself over the railing, her arms full of bangles, clacking against the wood.

"Isn't it amazing?" I continued to gaze out at the view.

"What?"

I turned to stare at my friend. "The view. The lake. This place. It's magical, don't you think?" With both hands on the rails, I tipped my head back and inhaled deeply.

"I think you've lost your mind." Sue Ann laughed. "It's the lake. The same lake it's been every summer since we were kids."

"Sue Ann!" I didn't bother hiding my exasperation. "We're not kids anymore."

"And?"

I sighed dramatically and rolled my eyes. "I've decided that it's time to grow up."

"We *are* growing up."

I spun to face my friend. "No. I mean like *really* grow up. It's time to get serious. No more little girl games. We need to start paying attention to the things that really matter in life."

Sue Ann scrunched up her nose and shrugged. "Like the view?"

"No, silly. Like *life.*" I held out my arms and spun around while my friend looked on in confusion. "I'm finally ready to understand what love feels like. And I *am* in love."

"With…"

"The lake." I was quickly growing impatient with my

friend's complete lack of understanding. "This place. I feel it in my bones. This place is special."

Her friend raised her eyebrows in question, so I continued.

"And now I want more. I want to feel the love of—"

"Don't say it." Sue Ann held up a hand. "Do *not* say a man."

"Why not?" I dropped my arms. "It's true. I'm done with boys. I'm ready for a man."

"You're done with boys?" My friend laughed. "How can you possibly be done with boys when you've never even had a boyfriend?"

Just because it was true didn't mean I wanted my best friend to point it out. Besides, Sue Ann was very quickly ruining my mood. I'd woken up on the first day of summer, ready to take on the world as a *woman*. Which, of course, meant I was going to need my best friend by my side. No one should be a woman on her own. Not when you were only eighteen.

"The reason I never had a boyfriend was because all the *boys* back home are just that—boys," I said matter-of-factly.

"I'm pretty sure there were men back home, too."

I ignored her. "Like I said. I'm ready for a *man*."

"Whatever." Sue Ann groaned. "I don't know about any *men*. But I'm sure hoping there are some cute boys at the dance tonight. I need you to help me pick which dress to wear. I have that black lace one that's just like the one Madonna wore. Or maybe the pink one. It's hot pink."

My earlier attempt at grown-up seriousness forgotten, I linked my arm through Sue Ann's and pulled my friend into the house and up to my bedroom, where we spent the afternoon trying on dresses, teasing our hair, dancing to Bananarama and dreaming about boys—or *men*—and giggling loud enough to earn more than one warning to be quiet from my mother before she finally kicked us out of the house altogether and sent us down to the lake to play.

As it turned out, as mature and serious as I'd been about being in *love* with the place, I still wasn't too old to run and jump off the dock the same way I had every summer previously.

Read the rest of Our Forever Moment now!

About the Author

Elena Aitken is a USA Today Bestselling Author of more than sixty romance and women's fiction novels. The mother of grown-up twins, Elena now lives with her very own mountain man and two dogs in the heart of the very mountains she writes about. She can often be found with her toes in the lake and a glass of wine in her hand, dreaming up her next book and working on her own happily ever after.

To learn more about Elena:
www.elenaaitken.com
elena@elenaaitken.com